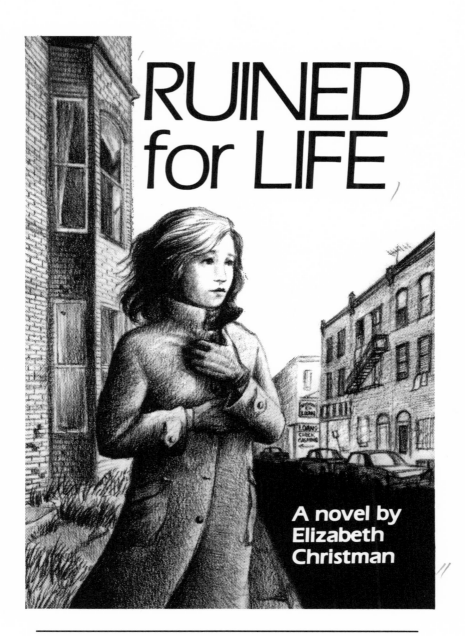

RUINED for LIFE

A novel by
Elizabeth Christman

Paulist Press ◇ New York ◇ Mahwah

Library of Congress Cataloging-in-Publication Data

Christman, Elizabeth.
    Ruined for life.

    I. Title.
PS3553.H74R8   1987   813'.54   87-8934
ISBN 0-8091-0395-8 (cloth)

Published by Paulist Press
997 Macarthur Boulevard
Mahwah, New Jersey 07430

Printed and bound in the
United States of America

A.M.D.G.

Ruined
for
Life

1

"*How* did I get into this?" Neal asked herself more than once during the retreat weekend.

"This" was the Company of Barnabas, an organization of recent college graduates who had pledged a year of voluntary service to the poor. The retreat weekend, in a rambling old compound beside a Wisconsin lake, was to give the twenty-five volunteers a chance to reflect on the mission they were about to undertake and to share their reflections.

It was late July. In mid-August they would move into their community apartments in five midwest cities. They would have jobs with social agencies, and would earn a volunteer's stipend of about four thousand a year. Pooling their stipends, five or six of them to a group, they'd live simply, and share their material goods and their experiences. Their lives, at least for this year, would challenge, as their handbook put it, "the rampant consumerism of modern society." They would "redefine their own values."

Cornelia O'Connor badly needed to redefine her values; she acknowledged it. She had been a rampant consumer all her life. Her father often vowed, writing checks for her bills, that there was no woman of any age in the city of St. Louis who could run up bills faster than Cornelia O'Connor.

"Yes, I'm a rotten spoiled kid," Neal often jauntily confessed.

But during her senior year at the University of Notre Dame she had begun to be troubled that she was living a life of utter selfishness, in the midst of a world of misery. She had had just a flashing glimpse of that miserable world when she tutored a child from a South Bend slum. Three Notre Dame students in a van picked up their pupils from dilapidated houses with junk-filled yards and took them to the tutoring center. The children were failing in public school because they couldn't learn to read. Neal's pupil was a pale, skinny, nine year old girl whose breath was bad, probably because she didn't get enough to eat. Her immensely fat mother often sat on the porch in the September afternoons drinking Pepsi. She never said anything to her daughter as she skipped off to the van, but simply watched impassively. There were several younger children in the family, also skinny and dirty. Once when her pupil did not respond to the van's horn, Neal had to go up to the door to summon her. She saw through the door the squalid room with the blaring television set, and the massive mother sitting before it with her can of pop. The weather had turned cool but LaVerne had no jacket or sweater. "Here, take this," Neal said, stripping off her own sweater. "Keep it. It's yours." LaVerne kept it. In only a week or two it looked as though it belonged to her: dirty, with pulled threads, missing two buttons.

The poverty of the homes she saw preyed on Neal, and, more than the poverty, the witless inertia. Those scenes ate at her comfort and goaded her to investigate groups at Notre Dame that were "socially concerned." One of her fellow tutors induced her to take part in a seminar with the theme "Feed my lambs."

"God didn't give us our talents and our privileges just so we can climb the corporate ladder," said the seminar leader. "He gave them to us to build a world where everybody has enough to eat, and dignity, and peace, and fair treatment." An impossible world, thought Neal.

One young man who was getting a degree in architecture spoke about city housing. He maintained that most "projects" were sterile and inhumane. He wanted to build humane dwellings for the poor. But first he had to understand the poor. He was going to join the Company of Barnabas, an organization of young lay workers run, rather loosely, by the Ignatian Fathers. Another man had been accepted at Harvard Law School, but had got a deferment for a year. He also had signed up with Barnabas. "If I'm going to work for justice, I'd better find out what it means," he said.

Neal, who had been applying to law schools herself, was fired by these statements. She looked into the Company of Barnabas. She liked the idea. She applied. "My parents have given me everything I wanted," she told the screening committee. "My values are totally materialistic. I've done nothing but take. I want to give."

She honestly did want to, but she found it hard to express herself in the approved terms, especially to her astonished parents. It seemed falsely pious to say that she wanted to follow Christ, and even more pretentious to say that she wanted to build a just world. Maybe it was guilt for her fortunate life, or a yearning for novelty and adventure, that pushed her. She feared that the kernel of honest unselfishness in her motive was very small and cheap.

Still she had persisted. She had signed up with the Company

4

of Barnabas. Now she was here at the July retreat, already wondering if she had made a mistake. All this "reflecting" and "sharing" and "openness" was making her squirm.

She had been assigned to the Chicago community, although this was not absolutely settled. One of the purposes of the weekend was that the members of the communities should test out their congeniality. The assignments could still be changed, or even cancelled, if some mismatch of personalities came to light.

The first night of the retreat was a general meeting. Father Jack Moran had said Mass in the big dining room of the main house, and then they'd roasted hot dogs on the lawn until the mosquitoes drove them indoors. Then they'd settled down on couches and wooden benches and on the floor to hear Father Jack and Sister Shirley describe the spiritual and temporal goals of Barnabas communities. There was a great deal of talk about simple lifestyle. They were to affirm their fellowship with the poor by living among them and living *like* them, insofar as that was possible. Their simple living was also to foster in themselves an awareness of how much unnecessary consumption of resources they were used to, and how much less they could get along on.

"Does this mean," asked a skinny fellow lounging against the wall, "that we shouldn't bring a stereo?"

Father Jack and Sister Shirley didn't seem to want to lay down flat rules. Each community should decide for itself what simplicity meant.

"What about a hair dryer?" The girl who asked this seemed a little abashed at her own question. "Hair dryers really save time," she added weakly.

There was a babble of discussion. Various appliances from color television sets to vacuum cleaners could be readily appropriated from parents and would be no expense to the community except for a few cents of electricity. What was the point of giving up conveniences that cost nothing? Some argued that that was a sort of artificial poverty. Others pointed out that the purpose of living simply was not primarily to keep costs down but to realize, and help others realize, that *things* were unimportant compared to people.

A stocky freckled young man sitting on the bench with Neal mastered the discussion with an appeal to symbolism. "An expensive stereo system is an acquisition symbol," he declared in a penetrating, edgy voice. "It stands for discretionary income—lots of it. If we want to understand the poor, we've got to get rid of symbols

5

that separate us." He apparently had said the definitive word. All over the room people nodded; Father Jack shot the speaker a look of muted approbation, obviously pleased that this consensus had been accomplished through discussion rather than by fiat. Neal read the name tag of the persuader: C. J. Bruckberger. So he was one of the group who would be with her in Chicago. She felt suddenly pleased, as though her team had scored a point.

Before they went to bed they prayed together, and a young man across the room from Neal led them in singing a psalm, while he played a guitar accompaniment. Neal found herself unexpectedly moved by the voice and the song—or was it the setting, the shadowy room lit by a few chunky candles, the hushed crowd of young men and women?

Yahweh, I know you are near,
Standing always at my side;
You guard me from the foe and you lead me
In ways everlasting.

That was the refrain. The singer nodded for them to repeat it with him. Between repeats, he sang several verses.

Where can I run from your love?
If I climb to the heavens you are there.
If I fly to the sunset, or sail beyond the sea,
Still I find you there.

His vibrant voice, the richness of his low tone on "there," the elegance of his phrasing, made Neal's eyes sting. She felt carried out of herself, far away from all silly concerns about hair dryers and stereos, lifted up to some exalted, unfamiliar plane. A spiritual plane, surely. Or was she falling in love with the melting voice of the singer, and with his luminous smile across the dim living room?

Later, lying on her cot in a six-woman dormitory, she asked the others: "Who was that guy? The one who sang."

Nobody knew his name.

The next morning after breakfast the groups met separately. The Chicago group was assigned to a porch outside the dining room, and they were all there when Neal stepped out. Sitting on a wicker settee was the man who had sung; he was Jake Traherne and he was

6

to be part of the Chicago community. Sister Shirley was there, too, and she introduced them all to one another: Maggie Rider, Neal O'Connor, Leo McGrath, Jake Traherne, and C. J. Bruckberger. They looked around at each other, smiling, friendly, curious, a little wary. Neal sensed the realization dawning on them all, as it was dawning on her: the romantic theory of a group of brothers and sisters living in a community of service to God's poor was about to become a concrete fact.

"Some of you know each other," Sister Shirley said. Maggie Rider and C. J. Bruckberger had both gone to Cambridge State University, but hadn't really known each other, C.J. explained. He knew Maggie's boyfriend, John Sims. He and John had worked in campus ministry together.

Leo McGrath and Jake Traherne knew each other well, having been at St. Isaac's together. Cornelia O'Connor, from Notre Dame, knew none of them. But by the end of the day, Shirley assured them, they were all going to know one another, and not just superficially. They were going to open themselves as deeply and honestly as they could, sharing their hopes for the year to come, their misgivings, their prejudices, their faults, their needs. It was terribly important for them to be utterly frank with one another today, while adjustments could still be made.

"Jake, if you don't mind, we'll begin with your situation," she said. In the morning light Neal saw that his face was narrow, sharply angled, intense, with deep-set eyes rather near together. "Jake was accepted into the Company of Barnabas after some soul-searching—on his part and ours." Sister Shirley spoke deliberately, looking hard at Jake. She obviously wanted him to pick up the burden of explanation, and he did.

"I have artificial legs," he said. The sentence lay there in stillness among them. Neal fell out of love with him. Jake waited for them to take in what he had said, and then continued. "I smashed up a car about three years ago. And myself with it. I lost my right leg below the knee, and the left one mid-thigh. I had to stay out of school two years. Surgery, and healing. And then getting the prostheses—the artificial limbs—and learning how to use them. I went back to St. Isaac's for my senior year and graduated. I can walk. I have elbow canes, as backup, but I hardly ever need them. I can climb stairs, if I have to. It just takes me a little longer."

He told this in matter-of-fact tones, which did not assuage Neal's queasiness. She kept her eyes on his face, not wanting even

7

to glance at his legs or attempt to imagine what combinations of plastic and metal and maimed flesh his slacks must conceal.

"He can do anything," Leo McGrath said. "We worked together in CILA at St. Ike's. He'll be an *asset*."

Sister Shirley pressed for a tougher examination. Leo's support was welcome, was generous, but they must all search themselves unsparingly to bring out whatever objections and misgivings they might feel. Neal's emotions were uncomfortable. Misgivings? That was a mild word. Jake's revelation had given her a shock she couldn't quite account for. Why should she feel this abhorrence, instead of flowing with sympathy and admiration for a man who had overcome such a frightful mutilation?

"You must open yourself, Jake," Sister Shirley went on relentlessly. "You must express your needs. Your sisters and brothers must know what your special requirements are—physical, psychological, spiritual."

"I've got to have—" Jake hesitated and his voice shook a little—"I've got to have a room to myself. That's, I guess, a psychological need. I take my prostheses off, you know, when I sleep. I can't—I don't—I mean, I don't like anybody to see me like that. I don't think it would be good for you guys either," he added. His face was dark red but he managed a sort of smile.

"How big is our Chicago apartment?" Leo McGrath asked Sister Shirley.

"It's an old flat. Three bedrooms. And on the ground floor."

"Let me go on," Jake said. "A few other difficulties. There are some chores I can't share in. Like, I can't kneel, so I can't clean the bathtub or scrub. But I can wash dishes, and cook. It just takes me a little longer."

"Do you have to have special equipment in the bathroom?" This was C. J. Bruckberger's question.

"A sort of lattice bench that I put in the bathtub so I can shower sitting down." Neal averted her imagination from the process. "It's removable. Folds up. Not bulky."

"Do you need help when you shower? Or dress?" C.J. pursued.

"No. But it takes me *longer*. I keep saying that. Everything takes longer. You've got to know that."

Five people, Neal thought, in a crowded apartment with one bathroom. And one of them a cripple, horribly maimed. But what of it? She wouldn't see that—but she would know it—and she *might* see it some time—might have to—and the thought of it was making her flesh crawl. She felt bitterly ashamed of herself, and suddenly dubious of her right to be here. How could a person so squeamish deal with all the sights and smells of poverty? Surely this was all a mistake. She had better drop the whole thing, go back home, go to law school. She would devote her law career to helping handicapped people, she resolved, offering a desperate recompense for her cowardice.

She longed for a cigarette. She had a pack in her purse and there was no rule against it, but there seemed to be an unspoken agreement that Barnabas volunteers didn't smoke. They were all ecology-minded, health-minded, and budget-minded. During the retreat Neal had so far not seen a single person smoke, not even outside the house.

Sister Shirley had moved her focus away from Jake and was urging the others to express their own needs and problems. Maggie Rider began to speak, a thin girl with a small serious face and a heavy braid of dark hair down her back. She said that when she had signed up for the Company of Barnabas she had expected to be placed in the same community with her boyfriend, John Sims.

"I understand why it can't be. I've accepted it. Barnabas people are brothers and sisters, not people in love. But I'm going to miss John terribly. I already do." Her voice shook and she seemed to fight hard not to cry. "John's way out in Oakland. Two thousand miles away," she added.

"He's with Barnabas too?" asked Leo McGrath. He had a very gentle voice. Exuberant curls stood out all over his head and his eyes were kind and merry.

"Yes, he's going to do prison ministry." She pulled herself together. "I don't mean to feel sorry for myself. John and I are determined to make this a good year, even though we're apart. We want to serve. We're going to continue after we're married. We might go to Latin America as lay missioners."

She went on to say that she had majored in education, had spent a year in Mexico and become fluent in Spanish, and intended to teach the Spanish-speaking poor.

"One of *my* problems," Leo McGrath said with an abashed grin, "is that I've never lived with *girls*. I have no sisters. I feel funny when I think of your shampoos and perfumes and stuff sitting on the sink.

And your pantyhose and your—well, all the things that girls use, hanging up to dry. I've only seen these things on television ads. Really!" They laughed uproariously, welcoming the release.

Leo went on: "And I'm afraid I'll do crude things that you ladies won't like—like if I belch or something."

"Or fart," said C.J. He had stopped laughing. "Listen, we're going to be living together like sisters and brothers, right? In very close quarters. We'll see each other at our worst. We can't worry about being crude. Human beings are crude—even girls."

He was right, of course. He was apparently one of those people who always have the right answer. Neal itched to take him down a peg. "Where are these *girls* you keep talking about?" She looked around the group. "Maggie and I are women, and so is Sister Shirley. I find it insufferable to be called a girl."

"Right. Right. Right." C.J. nodded his head about a dozen times. "I apologize. I'm a macho slob but I'm trying to overcome it. And another thing: I'm bossy and high-handed." He seemed proud of this. He intended to go into politics, he told them. The way to fight injustice and oppression was to change the civic structures. He had majored in economics and political science, and had worked for the Democratic Party in Ohio. His father was a state senator.

"We're scrappers, we Bruckbergers," he said. "You have to be, in politics. But if I try to bully you guys, you can cut me down." His grin was ingratiating. "Just remember, when I start throwing my weight around, that my first name is Clarence." He repeated it derisively. "Clarence. That's why I use C.J. But call me Clarence if I need it."

Everybody had confessed something but Neal. "I'm a spoiled brat," she said. "When I'd go home on break my mother would bring me a cup of coffee in bed." She added with a bubble of laughter, "I don't expect any of you to do that." She told them she knew that sharing things would be hard for her, but that she wanted to learn to do it, was determined to learn. This wasn't going deep, though; this was the expected, the conventional admission from the privileged child of an upper-middle-class home. Probably any one of them could have said the same thing. Neal was not being candid—she knew it. She couldn't uncover the shameful fears and the disreputable objections that were agitating her.

Sister Shirley continued to press them to express any misgivings they might feel about having a handicapped person in their household, any difficulties they might foresee.

10

"If we're trying to be open, why talk about a handicapped person?" demanded C.J. "That's a euphemism, isn't it? Jake, how do you feel about my referring to you as an amputee?"

Neal cringed. Even Sister Shirley looked startled. But Jake gazed steadily at C.J. "I accept it. I think you're right. How do you feel about having an amputee living with you?"

C.J. gave a series of satisfied nods. "I can handle it."

Sister Shirley, after her breathless moment, was delighted. "That's just great. That's real honesty!" That's brutality, thought Neal. "Now I'm going to leave you alone, to continue sharing."

There was an abashed silence after she left them. Leo broke it, with an apologetic chuckle. "Hey, this is *heavy*. But we're going to have some fun, too. All right?" They nodded gratefully. "Our own music—you heard Jake sing—and I'm a pretty good cook—"

"I can make deep-dish pizza," Maggie offered.

"And I can eat anything you can cook," declared C.J.

Neal joined the smiles but she couldn't think of any way she could promise to contribute to the "fun." She felt detached from them. Sisters and brothers? It seemed impossible.

"What if the place catches fire some night?" C.J. asked Jake. "How long does it take you to get hitched up?" Neal recoiled from his abrasive voice and his rude question.

Jake answered that it took five or ten minutes. C.J. shrugged. "What the hell, Leo and I could carry you out. No problem."

Neal saw the muscle jerk in Jake's jaw. "Carry you out" was demeaning, both the phrase and the picture it created. Oh, the picture! Jake's deformity bared to all the neighborhood against the gruesome light of a burning building.

"There won't be a fire," Neal declared loudly. "We're all responsible adults. And we don't smoke. None of us."

She saw her last pack of Marlboros lying at the bottom of a trash container under the stairs.

2

They moved into the old flat in uptown Chicago in the middle of August. The former group of Barnabas volunteers had vacated it a week or two before, and had cleaned it as well as the shabby old place could be cleaned. It was meagerly furnished with couch-beds and old painted dressers with ill-fitting drawers and some handles missing. There were no rugs, no curtains, only torn window-shades. "We can put up sheets," Maggie said. But it turned out that there were barely enough sheets for the beds, and no spares. They'd have to wash and dry them at the laundromat and put them back on the beds. There was likewise the minimum of towels, blankets, pillows, mismatched dishes and flatware, and old pans. The appliances consisted of a toaster, an iron, a broom, and an old tank vacuum cleaner.

The closets were very small, and one room had no closet, only a curtain across a corner of the room. "That's all right. We're not supposed to have a lot of clothes," Leo said. He seemed to have brought all his belongings in one canvas roll. He had come on the bus from Corning, New York. C.J. likewise had only one piece of luggage, a large laundry bag. Neal saw him eyeing with disfavor the two suitcases and garment bag that her parents had unloaded for her. But Maggie also had two pieces of luggage, and Jake had even more, which Leo was carrying in from his car. Barnabas volunteers did not ordinarily have cars, but Jake had been allowed to bring his because of his physical limitations. It was a sporty low black job, equipped with hand controls. Some of the neighborhood kids were already studying it curiously where Jake had parked it, a few buildings away from their flat, in the only available space.

The ground-floor flat wasn't too bad, Neal decided. It was old and shabby and the paint was peeling, and the stove would never be clean again, but the rooms were large even if the closets were small. The living room had a nice big bay window, which made the room bright. Some exuberant bushes in the narrow front yard provided a green outlook.

Leo and C.J. took the room with the curtained-off corner. Jake took the smallest bedroom. Maggie and Neal dragged their luggage into the other bedroom, and giggled as they compared the size of the closet to the bulk of their possessions. They'd have to try to shove their suitcases under the beds, with some of their contents inside. For the time, they could keep their winter clothes packed. The room's one window looked out on a brick wall about a foot away. "So we don't have to worry about curtains," Neal pointed out.

The bathroom looked like a comic stage-set when they had all moved their bottles and cans and brushes and tubes into it, crowding the medicine closet, the window sill, and the tank-top of the toilet. Jake's bathtub bench, folded up, wouldn't fit under the sink, and had to stay in the tub, to be removed temporarily when somebody else was taking a shower. There were only two small towel racks. "We'll have to get some more," Maggie said.

C.J. vetoed this, and Leo supported him. "Poor people don't even have a *towel* to themselves, let alone a rack," Leo said.

"I'm not sharing a towel," declared Neal. "Or a toothbrush. That's carrying community too far."

No, Leo didn't mean that. They'd each have a few inches of towel rack. Carefully he measured out each one's space, and Neal, giggling, marked the limits with nail polish.

"You brought nail polish?" C.J. asked incredulously.

"To mark our towel racks, Clarence." Neal menaced him playfully with her little brush. "How would you like a red freckle?"

He laughed and backed away. But he had some other ideas for organizing their bathroom. Why should they have five tubes of toothpaste? They could all use one tube, then another, and another. "But mine is Ultra-Brite—" Maggie began, but she weakened before C.J.'s look of disgust.

"We can start with Ultra-Brite. And get around to Crest and Pepsodent in due course," he said.

"Sure, that's all right."

"And we don't need five cans of deodorant," he went on. "We can start with the Right Guard. And—"

"Now wait a minute," laughed Neal, snatching away her Desert Wind. "Stop taking liberties with my intimate functions. I'll use my own deodorant. I'll keep it in my own premises." She removed her hairspray too. And her La Douce shampoo. Then Jake said he'd keep his electric razor in his room, and *his* shampoo and deodorant. And soon they had all removed everything but their toothbrushes, and had agreed to use the same bar of Ivory soap, and go through the tubes of toothpaste one by one. Neal, arranging her things on one side of the dresser, confided to Maggie: "I haven't dared to admit it—I brought my hair-dryer."

Company of Barnabas had given them an advance to start their housekeeping on, and their first task was to take inventory and get up a grocery list. Their predecessors had left them various staples such as flour, sugar, salt, spaghetti, canned tomatoes, rice. A simple life-style, they agreed, dictated that they'd use powdered milk, canned juice, and of course margarine. Leo wanted them to do without meat.

13

"Entirely?" This was C.J.

"We don't really need meat," Leo said. "Any nutritionist will tell you. Vegetables, and grains, and fish—they give you all you need."

But fish, they found, was expensive—they were studying a throwaway from the supermarket. Chicken was cheap, and hamburger was cheap. Leo protested against beef of any kind: the grain that was used to feed beef cattle was taking bread from the mouths of starving foreign children. But they overruled him: hamburger was so quick, and they had lots to do, and it didn't make sense to waste their own energy on cooking when they needed it for their jobs and their community life. "We can't solve all the world's problems at once," Jake said. "Let's just tackle uptown Chicago."

He suggested that they take his car to the supermarket, and bring back the sacks of provisions in the trunk. Leo could drive, as he already knew how to operate the hand-controls. Maggie, who seemed to have the most domestic expertise, would go along. It was a two-seater, so only two could go. Jake himself would not go, because he wasn't good at carrying sacks or pushing carts.

C.J., whose unpacking and settling in was already accomplished, decided to jog over to the Foster Avenue Neighborhood Association, where he was going to be a community organizer, and check in.

"Do you need help with your unpacking?" Neal asked hesitantly when she was alone with Jake, not sure whether it was tactful to offer. Sometimes handicapped people resented solicitous gestures.

"No, really, I can manage this stuff," Jake said. He smiled at her so beneficently that she knew he wasn't offended. "Thanks though. I appreciate it." He moved toward his room with his clumsy gait. There was a slight clicking sound as he walked, which Neal was to come to know and almost forget, as of a gear engaging or—she didn't want to speculate about what caused the sound. Jake turned at the door of his room, supporting himself a little unsteadily against the jamb, still smiling at her, but a little more grave. "I think we're going to get along fine," he said. "We'll be a loving family."

Maggie cooked the dinner that night. First she put all the groceries away and reorganized the kitchen; then she started a spaghetti sauce which simmered for a couple of hours and sent out tantalizing odors. Next she cut up a French loaf and made garlic

14

bread. Then she carefully wiped off the plastic tablecloth, set out paper napkins and the mismatched glasses and jars. Jake helped her tear up lettuce and spinach for a salad. Then she set him to washing all the knives and forks in hot soapy water; the previous residents had left them "gooky," she said.

When they sat down together for their first meal, a low sun was slanting through the uncurtained bay window and lighting up the wall of their living-dining room. They reached for one another's hands, and C.J. said a prayer: "Lord, thanks for feeding us. Help us get strength from this food to do the work you've got for us."

"Amen," they chorused. C.J. did it well, Neal thought: plain and honest. She knew they'd take turns saying grace, and she'd have to do it some day soon. She hated having to say impromptu prayers; she always felt so phony. She was glad that C.J. had not established a precedent of fancy rhetorical addresses to the Lord.

Leo was pouring from a big jug of wine they had bought along with the groceries. They had agreed that wine would be served on occasion, but not every night.

"To the cook," Jake toasted. "Maggie, this spaghetti is *great*. Let's have it twice a week."

"And, Leo, I only used a half pound of hamburger for all this sauce. It's *almost* meatless," Maggie pleaded.

"I'll probably have two helpings," Leo said. "It's super. Listen, don't worry about what I said. I'm probably too extreme. My mom thinks I'm weird. She says I ought to be a Trappist or a Buddhist or something. But I'm not going to bug you guys. Where'd you learn to make spaghetti, Maggie? You Italian or something?"

"My mother was." And then Maggie began to tell them about her life, her widower father, her four younger brothers and sisters, the responsibilities that had fallen on her at fourteen. "I've been cooking for a family for seven years," she said.

"What luck for us!" exclaimed Neal. Then the other side occurred to her. "But oh God, what about when *I* cook? I don't know how to make anything but scrambled eggs—burned scrambled eggs."

"I can make lumpy mashed potatoes. And solid rice," C.J. said. "But it takes me all afternoon."

"Zucchini strata is my specialty," said Leo.

"Zucchini strata? What's that?"

"It's a casserole of squash and crackers and milk, with cheese on top. Meatless," he grinned.

15

"Horrible!" exclaimed Neal. "Please pass the garlic bread."

The garlic bread and spaghetti went round again, and they laughed a lot, recalling their various cooking disasters. Then they began recalling camping disasters and athletic disasters, and telling one another about their childhoods and their families and their college days. They came to know something of one another's pasts, as the jug of wine became notably lighter.

Father Steve Rota came to see them that evening, rang the bell, in fact, while they were still sitting at the table. Father Rota was their "support person." He was a professor at Loyola University and he was going to be a friend to them, drop in on them frequently, advise them when they wished advice about any spiritual or temporal problems. He'd say Mass for them once a week in the flat, if they wanted him to. "That's entirely up to you, though," he insisted. "You are a community and you make your own plans. I'm not here to *direct* you in any way, or even to suggest. Just to be available."

Of course they all wanted him to say Mass once a week. It seemed unanimous. But Father Steve wouldn't consider it settled. "Talk it over when you're alone. How could you say no when I'm sitting right here?" He'd come around again in a few days when they'd had a chance to get settled and then they'd see.

He fitted their names, which he already knew, to their faces, listening very intently to the little autobiographies he diffidently asked for. Then he gave them a little autobiography himself: he was thirty-four, an economist, came from Boston, had been in Bangladesh for two years. Neal softened toward him when she heard this last detail. At first she had thought him too smooth, too practiced, too ready with the accepted phrases of a good personnel director. But a man who had spent two years in Bangladesh must have depths.

After he left, C.J. carried the dishes to the kitchen and Jake washed them. "No sexual stereotypes, please," C.J. said, elbowing Neal out of the way when she tried to help. "You get your screwdriver and fix that door knob." So Neal scrambled through a box of rusty implements and found a screwdriver and tightened the knob on the bathroom door.

When the work was done, Jake shouldered his guitar strap and strummed the instrument softly. The rest of them gathered, sitting on the floor with their backs against the furniture, and hummed or

16

sang, interrupting themselves occasionally with reflections about the life they were beginning. Lots of their reflections began with "We must—" or "Let's always—" C.J. said: "We must come out with anything that bothers us, okay? No grudges." Leo said: "Let's try to think of each other. I mean, each other's peace, and so on, and each other's comfort, you know what I mean?" He laughed. "I know it sounds corny, but let's try."

They sang some songs that they all knew: "Out in the Street" and "Imagine." Jake's voice, supple and rich, led them but did not dominate. For a last song, Jake suggested Foley's "Dwelling Place," as particularly appropriate for their first night in their new home. As he began the verse, "I fall on my knees—" Neal felt a stab of chill. He can't really fall on his knees, she thought, surreptitiously glancing at his legs. He wore dark blue pants, but they weren't levis. Probably he had to have them made specially, roomy enough to accommodate whatever devices they had to conceal. He sat now with one leg bent, the guitar resting against the thigh. That must be the leg that still has a knee, she thought. The right one? Was that what he said? The left one was stretched out straight, resting on the heel of his stiff shoe. But that one would bend too, through some hydraulic or other action. She had seen him bend it to sit or rise, but she had never wanted to observe too closely the difficult movements of his sitting and rising. She knew only that he got a lot of lift from his strong arms and powerful shoulders.

They sang the refrain together: "May Christ find a dwelling place of faith in our hearts. . . . " They met one another's eyes as they sang, affirming a unity that seemed to go deeper than they could express in their own words. Surely Christ was with them, dwelling with them almost before they had asked, loving them beyond their knowledge. When the song ended with its quiet repetition, "rooted in love," Neal felt uplifted and reassured. Yes, Jake was right: they'd be a loving family. She went around the group and kissed each one good night.

Leo laughed delightedly. "Hey, I like this. I didn't know what I was missing, not having sisters. Come on, Maggie." Maggie followed suit, but she looked a little stiff and reluctant.

"Don't expect this every night," Neal warned. Perhaps Maggie thought it was flirtatious, or feared that John wouldn't like it. "Only on special occasions. Like the wine."

Then they all went to their bedrooms. Jake said that after

everyone had finished in the bathroom he would shower. It took him a long time, and he'd do it at night so as not to cause a traffic jam in the morning.

Neal lay wide awake in her bed, listening to the sound of the running water—it did take a long time—and the other unfamiliar sounds that signified her altered life. The city sounds of night came through the open window: tires screeched, a motor cycle revved up, rock music boomed from a near apartment, a raucous group of party-goers called out goodbyes, a cat screamed. Maggie's even breathing declared that she had fallen asleep at once, but Neal was so alert that she wished for morning. Here she was, living in a flat in uptown Chicago, with four people who were utter strangers, and tomorrow she would report to a job in an alcoholic treatment center where derelicts were brought in from the streets. She thought of her tranquil room at home, her big four-poster bed, the ruffled curtains at her windows through which a subdued light would shine from a gas lamp in the driveway. In August at home the only night sound would be the song of cicadas. She wondered if she would ever again fall asleep to that sound.

3

S t. Vincent's Center occupied an old three-story building next door to a warehouse on a street of shabby stores and tenements. It had once been a transient hotel, and was now rented by the St. Vincent DePaul Society as a treatment center for skid-row alcoholics. The executive of the center, surprisingly, was a tall middle-aged woman with thick pepper-and-salt hair, Joan Kinsella, who described herself to Neal as a "recovering alcoholic." Nearly every person on the staff, she said, was a recovering alcoholic. She explained that an alcoholic was alcoholic forever and could never be considered "cured."

"I've been on skid-row myself," said Joan Kinsella. "Down to the depths. I've been in the gutter." Neal found it fascinating to learn that this commanding, handsome woman in a smart green knit suit had a few years ago been scooped off the street, drunk and bleeding from a head wound.

She took Neal on a tour of the Center, showing her the neat but run-down dormitory floors where the patients were required to clean their rooms and be out of them by nine each morning. All the doors were open, showing narrow beds with mismatched spreads, and sometimes a few pitiful efforts at decoration and scrawny plants. "Interior decorating by the St. Vincent DePaul stores," said Joan briskly.

She showed Neal the "lecture room" where the patients heard lectures and saw movies and slide shows to help them realize the deadliness of their habit. This room was also the recreation room where they could watch television or play cards when no program of treatment was scheduled. There was also a "crafts room," where a few ugly pillows were being made out of foam rubber and mustard-colored satin. "People donate things to us and we do what we can with them," Joan explained.

There was a dining room connected by a pass-through counter to the kitchen. At the moment a fat cook was cutting up potatoes and throwing them into a big kettle of soup, and a gaunt old man was washing dishes. Joan introduced them: Dan, the cook, and Willie, the dishwasher.

"Dan is staff. Willie is a patient," Joan said. She didn't lower her voice. "Willie's in the second phase of treatment, getting ready to work again, but not yet ready to live outside." She motioned Neal to sit at one of the tables, and brought two mugs of coffee from an urn on the counter. She began to explain the three-phase program: the first three weeks entirely devoted to getting the alcoholic to concentrate on his deadly disease; the second phase, which might last months, helping him to find a job and resume his responsibility for himself and others; the third phase, lasting indefinitely, giving moral and psychological support to the recovering alcoholic in the outside world.

"You'll be working on the second phase," she told Neal. "You'll be helping these people, especially the women, to evaluate their skills and see where they can use them in jobs. You'll help them upgrade their skills. You'll do liaison with the unemployment office. You'll search out job opportunities wherever you can. We need initiative and imagination."

A young boy who had been nursing a mug at another table got up and refilled it and approached them humbly.

"Can I sit down here?" He looked about eighteen years old, with round rosy cheeks. "I'm really nervous," he said.

"Are you waiting for somebody?" Joan asked him.

"For Mr. Leahy. He's calling them up over at Detox."

19

Joan nodded. She explained to Neal that a patient could not be admitted to St. Vincent's Center until he had spent several days at the Detoxification Center to rid his body completely of the effects of alcohol.

"I want to stop drinking and get a job," cried the boy urgently. His words seemed honest and pathetic, but Joan looked at him coolly.

"When did you last drink?" she asked.

"Last night." He looked abashed, and then repeated even more intensely, "I want to stop drinking and get a job."

Joan nodded, and went on talking to Neal about job counseling. A man came out of an office down the hall and signaled to the boy, who left his coffee and hurried after him.

"He's so young," Neal said, watching him go. "I felt awfully sorry for him."

"Yes. A lot of people here wring your heart. But the first thing you've got to learn is not to let them play on your sympathy. Alcoholics are very good at that. How well I know! I was a master."

"But I didn't think—he seemed sincere about getting sober. Wasn't he sincere?"

"Maybe. He wants to get a job. He thinks drinking is keeping him from getting a job. That's mixing things up. When an alcoholic comes here, he has to start by concentrating on one thing, and one thing alone: his drinking. He has to recognize that he has a *disease*. His first and only task is to get over it. He can't think about jobs, or his family problem, or any other problem. Just his drinking. He's got to get that under control."

"But I should think," ventured Neal, "that having a goal like getting a job would give him motivation to stop."

"He has to stop because it's a *disease*. If you have cancer you don't say 'I have to get over it so I can get a job.' No, you take treatment or have an operation just to try to recover from the cancer— no other goal. It's like that with alcoholism. If you start mixing up your goals—I want to stop drinking so I can get a job or so I can be reconciled with my family—you tend to think the problem is solved when you've got a job or go back to your family. Experience has taught us this, here at St. Vincent's. So our first phase is nothing but *disease*. You've got a disease. Here's what it's doing to you. You can die of it."

Neal learned that she herself would be required to participate in all the lectures, films, and discussions. She'd spend her first three weeks going through the treatment with the other patients, just as if she were an alcoholic. Only after she had immersed herself in the program, and felt the pain and the guilt and the humiliation, would she be able to understand and help her clients.

"If you've ever been drunk in your life, even once," said Joan Kinsella, "you'll feel the guilt." Neal almost denied that she had. Drinking a couple of beers too many at a college party or too much champagne at a wedding or giggling unsteadily on the way from a bar—Neal had never called such incidents being drunk. But with Joan Kinsella's keen eyes piercing her defenses, she kept silent.

That very afternoon she sat through an hour-long slide presentation that demonstrated in gruesome color the deterioration in the livers of heavy drinkers. Then there was a discussion of at least another hour, led by a nurse at the Center, in which those present were made to feel these horrible changes taking place in their own livers. "Where is it?" asked an old man plaintively. "I don't feel nothing." The nurse indicated the location, and they all pressed and sounded themselves, as the nurse explained darkly that the effects of liver disease were not confined to the abdomen. Neal felt her stomach as the others did. The liver had been as abstract to her as the soul, and hearing about cirrhosis reminded her of catechism lessons long ago when she had learned how sin blackened and deformed her soul.

The discussion was unspeakably harsh. Neal wondered how they could stand it, these eleven men and three women who sat there humbled and beaten. Some of them looked undernourished, others were puffy and bloated, some noses were swollen, some cheeks were purple, many hands shook. What horrors they must have gone through to submit to this battering. "You have a disease. It's killing you," the nurse said again and again, and she urged them to echo it. "Now what does all this mean?" she kept asking one after another. They were supposed to respond: "I have a disease. It's killing me." Eventually they all said it, including Neal. She saw her liver already poisoned and festering from the beer and wine and whiskey of college parties.

"Our program probably seems awfully grim to you. Brutal even?" suggested Joan Kinsella when she called Neal back into her office in the late afternoon. "Yes, you feel shaken. Believe me, it has to be this way. Our clients are hard-core alcoholics. Most of them haven't been sober for years."

21

"It just seems—I mean, I feel shattered and I've only been here one day. Don't they get discouraged?"

"Shattered. Yes. They have to feel shattered. We want them to. They must be shocked into realizing what they're doing to themselves." Joan poured a cup of coffee for Neal from the thermos on her desk, and filled her own cup. "Alcoholics, Cornelia, have an enormous capacity for kidding themselves. Even one drink makes people easy on themselves. Haven't you felt it? After one, your self-monitor starts to weaken. You offer yourself another, and another. You're very friendly to yourself. You assure yourself that you'll know when you've had enough. You're perfectly in control. We alcoholics keep assuring ourselves that we're in control, even after we've lost our jobs, quarreled with our families—after we've stolen and lied and whored."

Her clear brown eyes under heavy brows looked steadily into Neal's face and caught the disbelief there.

"Yes, I've done it all," she said. "And I know that I'm capable of doing it all again. I'm not cured. I've still got the disease."

"Do you mean you still crave alcohol?"

"Yes. My body craves it. But with God's help I will never yield. Drink is death to me. I know that now—death. Our patients have to learn that drink is death to them. They already suspect it or they wouldn't even be here. Now we have to ram the message home so hard that they will never forget it."

"I don't think they'll forget it," said Neal, shuddering under the recall of loathsome colored slides.

"Some of them do. The craving is terrible. Just this morning over on Madison Street I saw one of our clients slumped against a wall, filthy drunk. Only six months ago he went through here, all the way, got a job, was in an AA group." She sighed heavily. "But you can't let failure get you down. Even a few months of sobriety is some kind of achievement, for a late-stage alcoholic." She sighed again, and then she shook her head as though to throw off discouragement. "At any rate, Cornelia, you've come to a place where you're really needed. You'll see a lot of pain. You'll feel it. You'll suffer. But you'll help some miserable people."

"I hope I can," said Neal doubtfully. The pain and the misery seemed much more certain than the help.

Joan Kinsella reassured her, citing the successes of previous Barnabas volunteers in guiding clients toward jobs and training. She told Neal that she should dress for the part, a professional woman. Tailored dresses or suits, she suggested, glancing at Neal's jeans, would help to establish her authority. She put together a stack of xeroxed reports and offprints while she was talking, for Neal to take home and read. Tomorrow Neal would go with one of the other workers to the U.S. Employment Service to get acquainted with that organization and meet the people there. That trip would take place after the morning's film, which would show how blood vessels were broken down as a result of alcoholism.

Neal felt broken down herself as she trudged back to the apartment in the August heat, carrying her package of reprints and pamphlets. All the volunteers seemed weary that evening. They sat around, wilted by the heat and by the sobering encounters with their ministries. Maggie made a pitcher of iced tea, and they shared their apprehensions.

Jake was working as a parish assistant at St. Stephen's. He was to teach Christian doctrine to children, form a children's choir, revamp the adult choir, and organize a Bible study group. But Father Corley wanted all the old hymns, "nothing jazzy." He had an old-style catechism, and he wanted the children to memorize a lot of the prayers and doctrines. Jake was discouraged by his wary, opinionated stance.

Father Corley might be a problem for C.J. too. He lent the parish hall at St. Stephen's to the Foster Avenue Neighborhood Association for its meetings, and he thought this gave him the right to butt into its actions. If he didn't approve of FANA's methods, he'd threaten to withdraw the hall.

"We're gonna have to educate this guy," C.J. said.

"It's not easy to educate a guy seventy years old," mused Jake gloomily.

Leo was working at a men's shelter and soup kitchen. The shelter had moved twice in six months, and was being pressed to move again. Every time the director managed to find an old building to house it, the neighbors would complain to their alderman. Nobody wanted a lot of derelicts coming and going and lounging about in the neighborhood. Right now an eviction order had been filed, and Leo's first job was to go up and down the streets searching for any old store or empty flat which they could move to.

At Maggie's "alternative school" one of the children had eaten chalk and another had taken off all her clothes and run out into the street.

Neal described the slide lecture on cirrhosis of the liver. "It's rated R—for repulsive." A weak joke was the best she could do.

Maggie called John in Oakland that night and talked for a long time in a low voice. Afterward when they were in bed Neal could hear her crying.

"Listen, Maggie, things will get better," Neal told her, hardly believing it herself.

"It's so hot! It wouldn't be so bad if—oh, I'm sorry. I'm a real mess. I'm keeping you awake."

"I can't sleep either. There's not a breath of air in this room." Neal got up and looked out into the hall. "Jake's got his door closed," she reported. "If only he'd let us open it—but I wouldn't ask him. We could get some cross-ventilation."

"He must be suffocating in that little room," Maggie said.

"Would you dare to ask him if we could open his door?" Neal asked.

"I couldn't. His privacy—no, I couldn't."

"Neither could I."

4

*T*hey began to settle into a sort of family life, trying to cope with the irritations caused by crowding and temperaments. Maggie was a passionate housekeeper, a perfectionist. She made them all feel guilty. She didn't complain about dishes left in the sink: she simply washed them. She was forever wielding the vacuum cleaner, and taking everybody's towels and sheets to the laundromat.

"But I don't *mind*," she would insist, when they protested. "I'm the one who wants things neat. So it's up to me."

She wanted the group to be very faithful to the schedule they had agreed upon for their communal life. They had decided that they would allot one night a week to sharing their experiences and praying together. It was to be Monday night. Father Steve would come and say Mass for them on Thursday night, and that would be a celebration, followed by a spaghetti supper with wine. Monday meditations were to be deep and serious. Or so they had planned it.

But interferences began to be frequent. Jake's choir wanted to meet for practice on Monday night. C.J. had to address a tenant meeting. They'd put off their "meditation night" and often would not reschedule it. Maggie was troubled that they couldn't manage to adapt their individual activities to a group schedule. She thought they weren't being serious enough about "community."

For Maggie, schedules and lists were a way of controlling life, and she tried to apply them in her teaching too. But the erratic children in Maggie's "alternative" classroom did not take to schedules or lists or structured activities. They preferred hysterical chases and outbursts of destruction. In a very short time the seven and eight year olds knew how to unhinge their methodical teacher. Maggie bewailed the fact that she had no gift for ordering people around. She didn't even want to do it. Conscience was such an important force in her own life that she expected everybody to respond to it, at least after a little prodding. "I want the children to be *considerate* of each other—be kind to each other," she would insist. "I want to guide them, not punish them." But her appeals to their better natures seemed fruitless. She often came home in despair and threw herself into cooking or cleaning.

She did far more than her share of the cooking, and here too she was a perfectionist. She followed recipes meticulously. Her Greek casserole required lots of steps: squeeze the moisture out of eggplant; trim the lamb of all traces of fat; peel the mushrooms; skin the tomatoes over a flame. Maggie didn't skip a step. She said that cooking helped her get calm. "It's the one thing I can do right," she would say bleakly.

Her roommates lauded her pies and her fried chicken and her deep-dish pizza. The rest of them had no such skills. Neal's standard menu was hamburgers and baked potatoes. C.J. was the breakfast cook: he got up early and made the coffee and mixed the orange juice. Those who wanted toast or cereal got it themselves. Jake could make bread, which produced a wonderful aroma, but took an endless amount of time. As he had warned them, everything he did took a long time, but they tried to be patient so that he could feel himself an equal contributor. He moved awkwardly, and he had a little trouble with his balance when he had to lift or reach. He washed dishes with painstaking care and left the kitchen spotless enough to satisfy even Maggie.

Leo's zucchini-and-cracker dish was vetoed by everybody at its first serving, so Leo's quiet campaign for meatless meals expressed itself in tuna fish salad or scrambled eggs. He laughed at himself, admitting that he ate the meat-based soup they served at the men's

25

shelter. "Maybe I'm kidding myself, but I think I *ought* to eat what's been prepared. Like if you guys cook meat, I'll eat it. Maybe this is crazy. But I wish, you know, that we'd sort of cut down on meat."

"That kind of thing makes you feel virtuous—that's all it does," argued C.J. "Doesn't do a thing for world hunger. Or even Chicago hunger. You've got to politicize people to get action against hunger. Or any other injustice. Hamburger is quick and easy to cook. Let's eat it. Let's not waste our energy on personal gestures."

Wasting energy was the great sin in C.J.'s canon. When a neighbor offered them her old ironing board and Maggie pounced on it, C.J. protested loudly.

"We don't need an ironing board. We can iron on the table— if we have to iron." He deplored all frills and pushed for utter simplicity.

Maggie argued that an ironing board was not a frill—even pioneer women had used ironing boards. Neal pointed out that it was a gift, and cost them nothing. But why did they have to iron at all, C.J. wanted to know. Their clothes were drip-dry. Ironing was a wrong use of energy.

"You have to touch things up," the two women insisted, and Jake agreed.

They kept the ironing board, but C.J. was not reconciled. He scoffed at the waste of time when he saw Maggie or Neal ironing blouses. Maggie would touch up Jake's shirts for him, and Leo's too. C.J. needled her about submitting to a sexist role.

"But I've got the iron hot," she cried in vexation. "It's so little trouble. Takes five minutes. This sexist stuff, it's too much."

"Aw, come on, Maggie, can't you take a little kidding?" C.J. gave her braid a yank, and coaxed a grudging smile out of her. But he forbade her to touch up *his* shirts. He seemed to like to look rumpled and torn as a signal that he gave a low priority to appearance.

Jake gave it a high priority. He had brought more clothes with him than any of them, and they were expensive clothes. Neal imagined his heartsick parents trying to make up to him for his maiming by buying him clothes, watches, radios, stereos, and his sports car. He spent a long time on his grooming. They could hear his shaver and his electric comb from behind his closed door in the mornings, and at last he would emerge, looking impeccable. The rest of them ran around the house with feet bare, in various stages of undress, but they never saw Jake except in his public state. They knew he wore short-leg pajamas, because they often pooled their laundry, but that was as close as they came to understanding his personal arrangements.

"Do you think it's sexist for me to iron his shirts?" Maggie asked Neal when they were alone. "I can see why he likes to look good. He feels so ugly underneath."

"C.J. must feel beautiful underneath," Neal giggled. C.J. sometimes went several days without shaving; he let his hair straggle almost to his shoulders, perhaps to make up for its being so sparse on top; he wore the same two faded T-shirts all the time, one on his back while the other was in the laundry. He jeered at Neal for wearing Calvin Klein jeans around the house and at Jake for the little alligators on his shirts.

"But I own these," Neal argued. "Should I go to Sears and buy some $5.95 polyester pants? Wouldn't that be a waste of money?"

"Should I rip out the alligators?" Jake asked. "Wouldn't that be a waste of energy?"

Disputes like this were a household staple, joking in tone, yet reflecting some real irritation.

They argued about money too. By the end of the first month their money was virtually non-existent. They had been given an advance by Company of Barnabas for household expenses until they should receive their first paychecks from their agencies. And the advance had to be repaid. Each one had a monthly allowance of sixty dollars: persons leading a simple life were supposed to get along on that sum. Toward the end of September they were squeezing toothpaste out of the last communal tube, and eating bread and peanut butter for dinner. Leo's mother sent him ten dollars in a letter, and he gave each of them two dollars. In general they were on their honor not to requisition funds from their parents—or from anyone—but they agreed that this was an emergency. Jake's car was running on empty, and he had to get a gallon of gas into it to drive over to the parish where he worked.

"The first thing I have to do when I get paid is to get a haircut," Neal said, running her hand under the hair on her neck. "And that will just about chop my allowance in half."

"In half?" Leo was incredulous. "What does a lady's haircut cost?"

"Probably twenty-five. Twenty anyway. So I exaggerated a little," laughed Neal.

C.J. simply stared at her. He didn't say anything. His look of disgust was eloquent.

"I'm glad I don't get haircuts," Maggie mused, fingering her thick braid. "My phone bill will take such a hunk—" She and John called each other constantly at the cheap hours, nights and Saturdays, but their conversations were long.

"I can't believe you're going to spend twenty-five dollars for a haircut!" C.J. burst out.

"What can I do? It's the going rate."

"What can you do?" echoed C.J. angrily. "Do nothing. Let it grow. You're poor, remember!"

"Listen, we get an allowance for personal things, don't we? What's it to you if I want to spend mine this way? I'm getting sick of your criticisms. I tell you—"

"I'm worried about your head—the inside of it," C.J. interrupted in his loud voice. "There's something wrong in there. You're really mixed up, babe. You're supposed to be experiencing poverty. Do you realize—"

"Don't call me babe!" ordered Neal furiously.

"Sorry." C.J. shrugged it off, but he moderated his tone a little. "Look, I'm offering you honest criticism. I'm your brother. That's what this community is about, no?"

Neal was too agitated to speak. Maggie twisted her braid as she glanced in distress from Neal to C.J. Jake reached over and put his hand on Neal's.

"Listen," he said with a diffident grin. "I can cut your hair."

"You can?" They all stared.

"I cut my own." His thick brown hair looked expertly shaped. "I have a little trouble with the back. Maybe one of you can help me with my back, when I show you how on Neal. Take a chance?" he asked her.

"Sure." She was still trying to bring her anger under control.

"I'll get my scissors." Jake started to lift himself into standing position.

"I'll get 'em," Leo said, forestalling him. "Where?"

"On the dresser." It was the first time that any of them had entered Jake's room. "And bring a comb."

They draped a towel around Neal's shoulders and she sat on the kitchen stool, which was a little lower than Jake's chair. First he held her head lightly in his hands, fluffing her hair and examining its patterns. Then he combed top layers and directed her to hold them aside while he trimmed the lower. The rest of them watched attentively. His hands and his smile and his carefulness soothed Neal's sore feelings.

"Now turn the stool," he directed, as dark feathers fell from his shears. "A little more. Your hair is beautiful." More feathers fell. Neal released the layers as he signaled.

"Man, you're an artist!" Leo exclaimed.

Finally Jake showed Maggie how to make the back dip a little at the nape, and then asked her to give his own nape the same trim. Neal ran to look in the mirror and came back delighted. Then Leo wanted a trim, and took his seat on the stool, with the towel around him. Jake said he had never done curls, but he combed and clipped with confidence. "Curls are really easy. Your mistakes don't show."

After Leo had been shorn and was happily surveying his new small head, Jake turned to C.J. in an offhand way. "Want a neck trim?" C.J. shrugged and took the stool. "It looks thicker when it's shorter," Jake said, snipping. A few blond feathers mingled on the floor with the dark ones of Neal and Leo, and finally Maggie got the broom to sweep them all up.

"Everybody looks so nice!" she exclaimed, brooding over them like an anxious grandmother. She hated it when they quarreled.

By the time they went to bed that night C.J. and Neal had managed to speak civilly to each other once or twice. But the tension had not really disappeared. The next night was Father Steve's night to say Mass for them, and as they ate spaghetti and drank wine afterward, a couple of sly references to ironing boards and haircuts came out. Father Steve got them to open it all up, and he listened while they thrashed it all out once again.

"Twenty-five dollars for a haircut!"

"But I didn't spend it!"

"You were *going* to."

"Haven't I got the right—"

"You have to touch up shirt collars—"

"What's wrong with trying to look nice?"

"Shouldn't we at least have a couple of meatless days?"

Their heads kept turning to Father Steve. But he wouldn't issue any verdicts. They had to work out all these conflicts for themselves, he said. That was the meaning of community. "Don't concentrate on your disagreements," he urged them. "They're trifling. Concentrate on your great agreement. You're following Christ together. Think about that. The other stuff will sort itself out."

"He's right," C.J. said after Father Steve had left. They were all in the kitchen. Leo was scraping away at the spaghetti kettle and Maggie was gathering up plates. "I don't know how we got into this bickering. I take the blame. I want you guys to forgive me. Neal, you especially. I'm sorry I needled you about your hair. I'm an arrogant son of a bitch."

It was so unexpected for C.J. to be humble that they were all startled for a minute. Then Maggie stopped cleaning up and stood with her head bowed over the stack of dirty plates. "I need forgiveness too. I know I drag you all down. I'm really a drag. I get so discouraged, and I spread it all over the rest of you."

Jake jerked himself around and threw his arm over her shoulder, wet suds spilling down her sleeve as he hugged her. Neal leaned over and gave C.J. a zesty kiss on the cheek. "Thanks for shaking me up!" she exclaimed, breaking the solemn mood. They all laughed and resumed their cleanup. As C.J. turned away to cram the trash down into the plastic bag, Neal glimpsed the fiery blush that had suffused his face and neck. He had the kind of fair freckled skin that flushed easily and betrayed things in spite of his self-assured manner. What was this blush betraying? she wondered fleetingly.

5

Neal's assignment at St. Vincent's Center was chiefly to help women in the second phase of the program find jobs or improve their qualifications so that they could find jobs. Besides her liaison with the U.S. Employment Service, she made calls on employers who had shown themselves willing to cooperate with the Center. She constantly tried to enlarge the number of such employers, but it was hard work. Most of them would tell her bitter stories about alcoholics they had hired who had soon relapsed, wasting the training they had been given or leaving a botched job behind them.

"Once a drinker, always a drinker," said the manager of a printing company. "You're wasting your time, young lady. You can't save those sluts. Now, I'll be glad to give *you* a job—"

Neal held back the angry retort that almost escaped her. She must not make enemies. The Center needed the good will of employers, neighbors, employment agencies, and schools.

The Ferguson Business College, a few blocks from the Center, was one of the connections she had to cultivate. Mr. Ferguson had accepted two women alcoholics for typing courses, with free tuition. One of them had gained some modest proficiency and had gotten a job, which she still held. She had come back several times to see Mr. Ferguson and to thank him, and this had gratified him almost enough to make him forget the other woman, who had returned to drinking and stopped coming to class, but kept haunting the doorway of the school and begging for handouts.

Neal had another candidate she hoped he would accept. Janie Rawls was a girl of Neal's own age, though she could have been taken for thirty. She was so short and squat as almost to seem grotesque, with heavy shoulders, a big head, and short legs. Her face was dominated by a large nose and a low forehead, usually creased by a frown. Neal thought she had never seen a homelier woman, and yet she felt for Janie more than for any other client because of her youth. It astonished Neal that Janie should have lived through such turmoil during the same span of years in which she herself had been going to parties and football games and writing term papers.

Janie Rawls came from a good family, not unlike Neal's own family, in a Milwaukee suburb. Janie's story, as she told it to Neal, was that her parents were horribly ashamed and embarrassed by her ugliness. They had hoped she would outgrow her odd shape. When she was in her early teens they had considered an operation, or a series of operations, to lengthen her legs. An orthopedic surgeon had proposed bone grafts and skin grafts and plastic inserts that might add two or three inches to her height. But the cost would have been astronomical and the outcome was not at all certain. They had decided against it. "They gave up on me," Janie said. "They could hardly wait until I got old enough to go away to school. They wanted me out of sight."

She had gone to Northwestern. Being unloved at home and unpopular in high school was nothing to being an outcast on the campus. At home she had had a place to go, a younger brother and sister, a family dinner table, relatives, life around her. At Northwestern she lived in a single room in a dorm, attended classes, studied in the library, ate by herself and went to movies by herself.

"But did you try to make friends?" Neal asked gently.

31

"One night I asked sixteen different people to go to a movie with me. Would you believe that? I counted, just for the hell of it. They had already seen it. They had a paper due. They had a date. They were tired. They didn't have any money."

Janie had found comfort in alcohol and then in drugs. Drug users were a group, a fluctuating group but still a group, and there was a satisfaction in belonging somewhere. For most of her freshman year, Janie had continued to attend classes, but as she had drifted deeper into addiction, she had abandoned one after another of her courses. She didn't write or call her parents. When her grades were mailed home, all failures or withdrawals, her father came and searched her out and got her into a rehabilitation program. But he issued an ultimatum: she must not come home. He didn't want her infecting her younger brother and sister. He would pay her bills at the rehabilitation center; after that he would pay her expenses for another semester at Northwestern. Only one. Sink or swim, she must take charge of her own life from then on.

She tried again. In the fall she was back in the dorm, a second semester freshman, resolutely avoiding the drinkers and the drug-takers. She was utterly alone. As the winter closed in and her dorm window rattled, she would think of home, and the fire burning in the family room, and her little sister doing her homework on the floor. One night on her way back from the library she stopped at a liquor store and bought a bottle of sherry. A glass of sherry gave her comfort and helped her feel warm and forgetful. Two glasses made the comfort last longer.

Bars gave comfort, one especially. Flo's Place was a little neighborhood bar, frequented by Northwestern students.

"I'd limit myself to one beer, and I'd make it last," Janie said. "I'd try to kid myself that I was part of campus life. I'd talk to people a little. You know, just bar talk, nothing meaningful. It was very dark in Flo's, so—" She shrugged. Sitting down so that her grotesque shortness was not so obvious, in the dark bar which was merciful to her face, Janie had a skimpy taste of comradeship. She'd have a second beer to prolong it.

It was such a commonplace story. After her few weeks at the Center Neal already recognized it as the story of every alcoholic: the personal anguish of whatever kind which must be dulled with drink. The need for more and more drink. The drink which seemed to diminish the problem but actually made it bigger. The money running out. The narrowing of the world to the single pursuit of alcohol. The occasional frightful glimpse of reality. Self-esteem shrinking to no more than a dim filament, and then flickering out altogether.

"I was in jail three times. Shoplifting. There was a guy who would sell the stuff for you. Cosmetics, mostly, that was my specialty. In jail, I'd make up my mind to quit. But after a while—" She had lived this way for nearly three years: in jail, on the street, in a rooming house. She had not been in touch with her family at all. A parole officer had referred her to St. Vincent's. She had been through Phase I of the treatment.

"I've got a disease. I've finally recognized that," she said. "I'll always have it. Nobody can protect me from it—no doctor, no daddy, no priest. Only me. I have to fight it myself. I can never take a drink. Not even a sip. And I won't."

She was harsh to herself. She didn't ask for pity or sympathy. She was determined to get a job, to support herself, pay her debts, be an independent, self-respecting person. When she could afford it, she would go to college—"but not Northwestern"—and take up some profession, maybe nursing. But that was years ahead. The future she envisioned for herself was bounded on all sides by hard work, discipline, and solitude. The first step to self-support was to learn to type.

Neal was sure that Mr. Ferguson would take her into his business school, and after he interviewed her he accepted her. It was impossible to doubt her absolute resolve to stay sober. She was bright, too, and he placed her in a bookkeeping class, as well as the typing class. She spent all her free time at the Center working at her bookkeeping problems. Neal was haunted by the severity of her self-discipline.

"She's so young. Only our age!" she told her roommates at home. "The things she's been through. We just have no idea what people go through."

"We've been so *protected*," Leo agreed. At the men's shelter he was shocked every day by the filth, the disease, the abandonment in which some people lived. "One old guy told me today that he has not slept in a bed one night since last March. He was *laughing* about it. He said he knows all the best places to sleep free in Chicago. He was really funny—said he's going to write a book about it and get American Express to publish it."

33

"What gets me about Janie is that she's so alone," Neal went on. "She has nobody. Not a single friend. And she's only twenty-two."

"Why don't you bring her over some night for dinner?" Leo suggested.

Neal looked around at the others, pleased but uneasy. "How would you all feel? I don't even know if it would be allowed. And don't forget—how can I say this?—she's strange-looking. You might say, even a little deformed."

"What of it?" asked Jake, almost angrily.

"Well, nothing. I only meant—" Neal was flustered at her own tactlessness. She had simply wanted to prepare them for Janie. "We couldn't have wine that night, though—" she hurried on. "She can't drink, you know." They seldom had wine anyway.

"Alcoholics have to be able to refuse a drink when other people are drinking," said C.J. "You can't coddle them."

"Maybe I could help her," said Jake. "About her looks, I mean. Show her how to put her best foot forward—so to speak." He flashed Neal a little grin, self-mocking and apologetic.

"You *could!* So is it all right with you guys? If Miss Kinsella says I can invite her?"

"I'll make deep-dish pizza," promised Maggie.

"Hey, let's have her tomorrow!" cried C.J.

But Joan Kinsella shook her head when Neal proposed the invitation.

"No, I wouldn't do that, Neal. Not a good plan." She seemed to expect Neal to drop the idea, perhaps in relief. "Don't you see it yourself? It's unrealistic. You'd offer her a peek at a life that she can't share—at least for a long time. Offer a crumb of friendship that you couldn't follow up on."

"Why couldn't I?"

"And besides that, it wouldn't be good for the other women you're working with. If you invited Janie to your home, Mamie Schorski would expect to be invited, and Mrs. Healy, and Betty Grubb. We don't want to show favoritism."

"But Mamie and Betty are *old*. Well, older anyway. But Janie is my age. I don't think those older ladies—"

Joan lifted a wry eyebrow. "They don't think of themselves as old. No, Neal, we don't want to give any special privileges."

"Why did you say I would be offering a crumb of friendship?

And that I would never follow up on it?" Neal demanded. "Why shouldn't Janie and I be friends—I mean, lasting friends? I don't intend to offer just a crumb and then drop her." She felt that Joan Kinsella was condescending to her, treating her service as a youthful fling at idealism, instead of a mature commitment.

"Neal, be realistic," Joan commanded, fixing her with those searching dark eyes. "You're a beautiful, rich, bright young woman. You've given a year to this work. I honor you for it. But you're only playing at poverty. No, wait a minute. Don't get angry. Let me finish. You've given a year. But after this year, you can do anything you want. You'll have your choice of men to marry, if you want to marry. You can go to law school or graduate school, or get a good job. What have you got in common with Janie Rawls? She has absolutely nothing to give you. Nothing! Friendship has to be two-way."

"You don't have to give *things,*" answered Neal passionately. "She has a lot to give me. A lot to teach me."

"Don't misunderstand. You can be friends in a certain sense. You can help her and learn from her. But as for taking her into your life, it can't be done. It would be dangerous to try. Dangerous for her, I mean."

Neal set her jaw. "I don't agree."

"I haven't seen your apartment, but I can imagine the scenario," Joan mused. "Four or five attractive young people, a stereo going, a spaghetti dinner, lots of laughs and in-jokes. Your roommates, of course, are caring people. They'll be warm and friendly to your guest, the homely little alcoholic who's trying to fight her way back to just the meager success of a typing course. They'll ask her about her typing course. They'll encourage her. That's about the only subject they'll be able to talk to her about. They're too sensitive to bring up her drug trips or her alcohol crashes. They won't talk about other derelicts and unfortunates that they are working with—it might offend her. The evening will be very awkward. And she'll feel it. She's sensitive too."

"It won't be awkward," said Neal stubbornly.

"She'll feel out of place. She'll feel even uglier and odder than she usually does."

"One of my roommates has no legs," announced Neal, thinking of Jake's offer to help Janie. "He knows what it is to be physically repulsive—" Then Neal halted, as a wave of confusion and shame engulfed her. She had never before said that Jake was physically

35

repulsive; she hadn't even expressed it that way in her thought. She was horrified at having applied the cruel phrase to Jake—and to Janie, too, by analogy.

"Think it over," said Joan coldly. "Janie has herself well in hand just now. But this is always precarious for alcoholics. She's slipped back before. Why interfere with this careful balance of hers?"

Thus Joan avoided a flat proscription and saved Neal from having to back up a determination that was already wavering. No, she certainly did not want to jolt the stern course of Janie's climb back to self-respect. And her own self-assurance was shaken by hearing herself utter physical slurs that she hadn't even known were in her consciousness. She had resented it hotly when Joan Kinsella had described her as rich, and as "playing at poverty." Those words had stung. But thinking them over, Neal began to suspect that her own notions of riches and poverty were silly and simplistic. She *was* rich. All the volunteers were rich, because they had so much self-esteem and talent and youthful happiness that they could afford to give away a year of it. Even Jake, legless, was pouring out spiritual energy and musical gifts for the parishioners of St. Stephen's. Janie Rawls was poor in more than a material sense because she had nothing to give. Her whole mind and will were concentrated on herself, on rebuilding herself. She had never asked Neal a single question about her own life.

She didn't participate much in the common life at the Center, either. The residents were supposed to help one another by sharing their experiences and their resolutions for the future. "Mealtimes are not only for bodily nourishment but for coming to know one another," said the rule sheet. "You are to be at every meal even when you don't feel like eating." Janie obeyed this rule grudgingly. She was contemptuous of small talk. Her ugly frowning face did not invite friendliness from others. She was obviously impatient to get back to her bookkeeping text, or to the paperback romance novels that she was incongruously devoted to.

Neal advised her to make more effort to be comfortable with other people. "When you get a job you'll have to socialize with the people in the office," she said.

"Why?"

"Why? Because—well, offices are like that. I mean, you spend eight hours a day with each other. Naturally you get to know each other. You make friends."

"I won't."

"Why do you say that? Don't you want to make some friends?" Neal remembered with a pang the college freshman who had asked sixteen people to go to a movie.

"I'm not counting on making any friends. I don't want anything from anybody. I'll take care of myself."

"But you can't go through life—I mean, personal relationships are part of life." Neal stepped carefully over this touchy ground. "Right now you're wary of people. I understand. But it will get easier. When you're out working you'll—well, you're so young. Someday you'll—" Neal stopped, unable to find a phrase that was both reassuring and honest.

"I'll what?" demanded Janie, her scowl deepening.

"Well, some day you'll probably get married," Neal said, trying for an airy tone.

"Are you kidding?" asked Janie so bitterly that Neal felt ashamed.

She admitted to herself that Joan had been right to advise against inviting Janie to dinner—for the present, at least. In fact, Janie would probably refuse to come. Neal couldn't reconcile herself, though, to Janie's view of her own future as totally isolated, self-contained, loveless. It was too terrible. It couldn't be, it mustn't be like that. There had to be some way for this ill-favored, forbidding young woman, carrying in her body the disease of alcoholism, to learn to give and receive affection.

Neal asked her sister and brothers to pray for Janie. They often prayed together for the people they were trying to serve. "Lord, do for them what we've failed to do," was C.J.'s way of praying. Then they would acknowledge the ways in which they had failed. "I can't stop Medgar from having these tantrums," Maggie said, "because I get so upset when he screams." She was distraught at the chaos of her classroom. Leo prayed for Alderman Lawicki, who was blocking the new shelter site on behalf of his constituents. Leo begged the Holy Spirit to instill compassion into the politician. When Leo himself had pleaded with him, the alderman had responded with an obscenity.

Neal prayed for Janie. "Lord, send somebody to her—somebody to love her. Find her a job where there'll be some kind person, maybe an older lady. And a good boss, an understanding boss, who will give her a little praise. And a couple of people her age—"

"Neal, why not let the Lord staff the office?" C.J. suggested.

Their prayer sessions often ended this way, with a quip from

C.J. He had a good sense of timing, Neal thought. He kept them from going on too long, into self-indulgent confessions of guilts and failures, or into over-elaborate petitions. "Don't give God instructions," he'd say. "He knows how to do it." Praying together was not as uncomfortable as Neal had expected it to be, with C.J.'s raillery to ward them from pious pomposities.

But common prayer didn't get very deep, Neal sometimes thought. When people prayed together they still kept something of their public personalities, their polite reticences, their civility. There were layers of shame and need that they never opened, because they had to spare others. Neal certainly could not acknowledge her shameful squeamishness about physical defects. She prayed in bed at night for more humility and more tolerance, and when Father Steve came over one night for dinner she managed to have a little time with him.

"I need grace," she said urgently. "I need help. I'm really rotten inside." She told him that trivial physical things affected her attitude toward people. "Honestly I almost loathe C.J. sometimes because he doesn't clean his fingernails. I'm not exaggerating, Steve." She laughed when Father Steve glanced at his own nails. "And the people I work with—if they're dirty, or if they smell—" She was circling around the subject of Jake.

Father Steve nodded. He knew what she meant. In Bangladesh the smells had been almost the hardest thing he had had to deal with. "And yet when you're away from them, you wonder why you made such a big deal of it."

"And the sights," Neal reiterated. "I know it's totally unimportant that C.J. has dirty nails, and greasy hair. And that Mrs. Schorski, my client, has a huge mole with hairs coming out of it, and—But I can't seem to ignore these things. And Jake. He's such a marvelous man, but I—"

"You can't even *see* his disfigurement." Steve did not say this argumentatively. He seemed to participate in her reflection.

"No. But—can you believe it?—I'm always conscious of it."

"It's natural. You're very young. You haven't seen much of the pain and horror in the world. You've been very sheltered."

"But what can I do about it?" Neal demanded. "How can I get over these horrible feelings?"

"You said it yourself. You need grace. Ask for it. Keep asking, okay?" He made the sign of the cross over her and murmured some words, as Leo came in from the kitchen and began to set the table.

"What's that?" Neal asked Steve in surprise. "Did I go to confession?"

"Yes. And don't forget that the sacrament gives grace."

"Hey, Leo, I just went to confession!" called Neal, laughing at the old feeling of lightness that she remembered from childish confessions.

6

*T*here were three ironclad proscriptions for alcoholics in treatment at St. Vincent's Center: no alcohol, no sex, and no gambling. All the other rules, and they were many, served these. Residents had to be up and dressed, with their beds made and rooms put in order and vacated by 6:30. They had house chores to do before 9:00. They had to attend all lectures, discussions, therapy sessions, and other activities. They were urged to get fresh air and exercise by taking walks around the neighborhood, but they had to go in twos or threes, the idea being that they could thus help each other avoid the bars and the parks and the companions from their drinking pasts.

They could play cards but not for money, not even for paper chits. They could watch television and read newspapers and books, but always in the communal recreation rooms. They were not allowed to be in their bedrooms during the day, or even on the bedroom floors. Even the mildest flirtatiousness between men and women was frowned on by the Center staff.

Most of the residents weren't up to this anyway. They were desperate people, driven to this harsh place because their lives were all but destroyed by their drinking. But a few of them seemed to have sparks of sexual appreciation smoldering.

Blaze Curry, watching Neal come down the corridor one morning, gave a short-long whistle, the age-old male signal of appreciation for a pretty girl. A staff-counselor, standing at the reception desk, jerked around to give Blaze a dirty look. Blaze Curry had once been a professional baseball player. He had a scarred, ravaged face, but his rolling, jaunty gait still recalled the lead-off hitter strolling toward home plate, swinging a couple of bats. At the counselor's rebuke, he crossed himself elaborately and brought his hands together before his forehead in a parody of repentance. As Neal passed him, trying not to laugh, she heard the murmur from behind his hands: "Hiya, Gorgeous." Neal exploded, and the counselor looked angry.

"But that's such a trifle," Neal protested later at a staff meeting. "Just a whistle."

Joan Kinsella and her staff were sticklers for the rules. They insisted that rigid discipline was a part of an alcoholic's recovery, rigid adherence to all regulations. No sex: that was one of the regulations. No sexual conversation, no sexual gestures or innuendos, no sexy magazines or posters—the Center was like a monastery or convent, Neal thought. It was almost inhuman.

"Not at all. It's *more* human," Joan claimed. "We encourage friendship, and helpfulness, and sharing. We want all participants to care about each other, support each other. See one another as human beings. Human beings, not sexual objects."

Neal saw the rightness of this, but it was hard to make fine distinctions. A pink-cheeked old Irishman, Paddy McGlynn, certainly over seventy, would beam upon Neal, leaning on his broom, as he cleaned up the dining room. "Ah, to be young again!" he would exclaim, his blue eyes twinkling. Was this a sexual innuendo? Neal decided not to mention it in the staff discussion.

"I'm surprised at you, Neal," Joan said lightly. "A champion of women's rights and dignity! I thought you'd be outraged at a whistle." The staff liked to tease Neal about her feminist position. In fact she was confused about her own attitude. She remembered how she had lashed out at C.J. for calling her "Babe," and for referring to her and Maggie as "the girls." Yet here at the Center she felt that they were all making too much fuss about styles of sexual address that were traditional with most of these people. Paddy McGlynn had grown up in a world where gallantry to young ladies was taken for granted, and was even considered proper and polite. Blaze Curry's whistle was the sound of his youth, when young women liked it, even if they tossed their heads indignantly. Neal felt vaguely that to squelch these sparks of male posturing was to diminish the little self-esteem these men had left. The lives of alcoholics in treatment were so stripped and humiliated, often so spiritless, that Neal almost welcomed—quite against her convictions—a wink or a whistle or a grin of appreciation. Joan insisted that little things led to big things. With men and women living together at the Center, the only way to guard against sexual trouble was to outlaw even the smallest verbal exchanges. Neal gave her assent, with secret reservations.

She saw Blaze Curry tweak a curl over Janie Rawls' ear one morning. "Hiya, sweetheart!" Janie jerked her head away angrily and Blaze chuckled. Nobody saw this but Neal and she ignored it. Later she noticed that Janie was more animated than usual when the group discussed a film about addiction. Janie made two comments in her gruff, aggressive style. She didn't look at Blaze but she kept winding a curl around her finger as she talked. The same curl he had pulled? Usually Janie sat bored and resentful and said nothing.

"By God, Neal, you're a sight for sore eyes," exclaimed Dan, the cook, when she came into the kitchen for a cup of coffee. She asked him to make her a cheese sandwich for lunch. "Anything for one of your smiles!" he answered. "Oh, to be young again!" cried Paddy McGlynn, wiping off the table where she sat down with her coffee. The silent, rheumy-eyed dishwasher glanced her way, and the corners of his stiff mouth lifted a little. Blaze Curry passed the door, bunched his fingers and kissed them, then glanced up and down the corridor in a pantomime of trepidation. Neal bent over her coffee. Surely none of this did any of them any harm.

"My feminist convictions are being tested," Neal said a few days later to her roommates. She had just had a phone call from Kevin Lindemann, whom she had dated two years earlier at Notre Dame. "Kevin is your total chauvinist, a jock of the worst sort. We fought constantly," she laughed. "Now here I am going out to dinner with him tomorrow."

"But why?" It was Leo who asked, but all their faces questioned.

"I don't know. Just for the novelty. It's so long since I've been wined and dined. We're going to the Cape Cod Room."

C.J. frowned. "The guy must be loaded."

"He's an accountant. Works for Arthur Anderson. I told you he's your typical success-oriented chauvinist. I think I'll order lobster."

"But why do you want to spend an evening that way, Neal?" Maggie asked. "With an *accountant?* What will you have to say to each other?"

"I won't talk. I'll just eat."

"You'll spend enough in an evening to feed a family for a week," C.J. said sourly.

"*He'll* spend it. Not me."

"How did he find you?" asked Jake.

"Oh, the alumni magazine. Domers always find each other."

"Domers?"

"You've heard of the Golden Dome? So everybody who goes to Notre Dame is a Domer. And Domers are always looking each other up."

But why did Kevin look her up? That was what Neal wanted to know. During their senior year at Notre Dame they had scarcely seen each other, after a tempestuous series of quarrels that covered such diverse topics as Reaganomics, Woody Allen movies, the Church's stand on divorce, and finally Neal's curly perm. Kevin thought curly perms looked "cheap." He told her she looked like a floozy. She denounced him as a bigot, an overbearing, conceited, narrow-minded, selfish, anti-intellectual, war-mongering pig. For good measure, she added an obscenity. His face closed in revulsion. That had ended the quarrel, ended the relationship. She had cried afterward in rage and hurt, and the wound had ached for a while. But now it seemed amusing to remember that her last word to him had been an obscenity—to Kevin who thought obscenity unpardonable in a woman.

She had been thrilled when Kevin first dated her. He was good-looking; he was a soccer star; he was president of the junior class; he had a self-assurance that didn't offend her because it was so good-humored. Looking back at her nineteen year old self she saw how conventional her attraction to Kevin had been. Kevin Lindemann was exactly the sort of young man every middle-class parent covets as a son-in-law, and every middle-class girl has been brought up to hope for. For nearly a year of football games, beer parties, dances, and spring break in Fort Lauderdale, they had laughed and capered. They had grown fond and possessive. Deep differences had begun to count. The quarreling had started, but with intervals of contrition and tenderness. The hostility had sharpened and the soft interludes became less frequent, and the parting had been bitter—bitter enough that neither had made a move toward the other the rest of the year, and even on graduation day they had looked stonily past each other.

Now Neal felt how silly and childish their rancor had been, and she blamed herself most for not having tried to salvage at least a civil friendship out of the shards. She even wished *she* had been the one to make the phone call. She couldn't imagine what had made Kevin want to look her up.

"To see if it was true," he said, facing her across the red-checked tablecloth in the Cape Cod Room. "I read that you had joined something called Company of Barnabas. I couldn't believe it. The good-time girl, the gorgeous coed—I had to see for myself."

"Kevin, you haven't learned *yet* not to say coed!" She laughed, showing her perfect teeth and her fugitive dimple. He looked marvelously handsome, leaner, a little older, tanned from skiing. It was suddenly exhilarating to be sitting down to dinner in a sophisticated restaurant, surrounded by diamonds and expensive perfume.

"Oh, hell, there I go!" cried Kevin striking his forehead. "Off on the wrong foot already. Let's start the scene over again. I wanted to see for myself if that intelligent, that socially-concerned woman—how'm I doing?" The headwaiter hovered, attentive and patronizing. Wasn't it just like Kevin to know the headwaiter by name? "How about champagne, Neal? For the special occasion?"

"Love it." The headwaiter beamed on them and signaled the order to a minion. "I work in an alcoholic treatment center," Neal added inappropriately.

"Really?" Kevin trimmed his smile. "What do you do?"

But Neal wanted to put that off until later. She was sorry she had mentioned it just then. She wanted to drink champagne, and study the sumptuous menu. "You can't imagine what a treat this is, after months of living at the poverty level. I won't look at the prices. I don't dare. I might get up and run."

"Poverty level. Why? I don't think I ever saw this side of you."

"I didn't even have this side then. I grew up a lot last year, Kevin. I changed. Listen, I was a nasty little bitch to you. I've been really sorry ever since."

"No, no Neal." He reached across and took her hand. "Not at all. I'm the one. I was a colossal jerk. But I've grown up too."

They held hands, smiling foolishly at each other, as the waiter came with the champagne cooler.

"To our new maturity," Neal toasted, giggling, after the wine was poured.

"Seriously now," urged Kevin, drawing his eyebrows together like a businessman who wants to know the bottom line. She was to explain exactly how she came to join this volunteer group, what she was doing at the alcohol center, what the point of it was, and what future she saw for herself. A, B, and C, and a concluding statement.

"Kevin, I should have made an outline. I'm not prepared. You first. Where do you live? What's your job like?"

"I've bought a little condo in Uptown. Just a studio. I travel a lot." Neal thought of Greece, Austria, the Caribbean, but it turned out that he meant Kokomo, Peoria, and Vandalia, where his company sent him for a few weeks or a month to do an audit for a local firm.

"Isn't that pretty boring?"

"The job is intense. There's no time to get bored." He spoke reverently of his work, the responsibility of it, the authority which his firm enjoyed.

"But at night?"

He shrugged. "The tube. I can nearly always get back to Chicago for weekends. In fact I'm working in Vandalia right now. Came in last night. Ready to make up for all those dinners at Howard Johnson's and Arby's." He opened the menu. "Come on, Neal, let's do this right. Start with oysters?"

Zestfully he ordered: oysters, crab bisque, lobster, asparagus vinaigrette. "And we better have another one of these." The bottle of champagne was nearly gone.

"I won't be able to tell about this at home," cried Neal, when the plate of oysters was set before her. "This orgy."

"Think of it as research. Doing your sociology. A site visit, isn't that what they call it? To a ghetto of the rich."

"I should have my clipboard." They studied the people around them, making up instant backgrounds and psychological pathologies. Board of directors, Sears Roebuck, frigid wife. Real estate tycoon, hypochondriac. Account executive, Leo Burnette, mother-dominated. Architect, publicist, jeweler, banker: all miserable in spite of their privileges.

"Or maybe *because* of their privileges." Neal narrowed her eyes and pointed her lobster cracker at Kevin. "Think of that, my dear colleague. Perhaps these unfortunate patients are so anxious and unhappy not because they lack some *je ne sais quoi*, but because they have—*everything!*"

"Eureka, my dear colleague! A breakthrough! We must cable at once to Dr. Freud."

They were back in the silly times at Notre Dame, the days of clowning and stunts and foolish "personals" in the campus daily.

Neal felt young and irresponsible again, and she exulted in the feeling. After the lobster and the champagne, and the sinful cheesecake, they walked down Michigan Avenue and ogled the windows in Water Tower Place. Then they went over to Rush Street to a nightclub where there was jazz and blues, and even a tiny dance floor.

As it turned out, she never did get back to telling Kevin about her work at the Center or her feelings about living with the poor or the other things he had wanted to know. The time and the mood were not right. Drinking brandy at five dollars a thimble while talking about poverty and injustice would be material for satire. "I'll have you over, and you can meet my housemates, and hear all about it." She had to yell it; the band was playing "When the Saints Come Marching In."

"Don't you love Chicago?" asked Kevin, riding up Lake Shore Drive in the taxi at 3:00 A.M.

Yes, she loved it. But a fleeting remonstrance flickered through the haze of champagne, brandy, jazz, and high spirits. This is not *my* Chicago.

"Shall I come in?" asked Kevin, when the cab stopped before the flat. "I'd like to see how you live."

"It's too late," said Neal. There was a light in their living room, but probably it had been left on for her. "I want you to come sometime, though. I'll invite you for dinner."

So he asked the cab driver to wait while he walked her up to the door. There was a long hug and a satisfactory kiss, and then Neal turned her key in the lock, and the cab drove away. There was no one in the living room, but when she turned off the lamp she saw a crack of light under Jake's door.

"Thank God it's Sunday!" she exclaimed the next morning, reaching into the refrigerator for the pitcher of orange juice. "What a pagan orgy last night!"

"Are you hung over?" Leo was scrambling eggs, while Jake was making toast.

"I *ought* to be. Considering how I ate and drank and rioted, I ought to be throbbing and retching. But actually those scrambled eggs look good. Is there enough for me?"

Leo wanted to hear all about her evening, including descriptions of the Cape Cod Room and Jeremiah's Jazzique. Jake listened but didn't say much.

45

Neal felt a sort of strain or hostility in all her roommates that day, except in Leo, who never seemed critical of anybody. Or was she imagining that they were critical because she herself felt guilty? Guilty of what? She wanted to talk to them about her adventure and domesticate it, but she was balked by their lack of response.

Father Steve came over in the late afternoon and said Mass for them, and stayed for supper.

"Neal was out with a big spender last night," C.J. told him. "The Cape Cod Room, Rush Street. Total hedonism, right, Neal?" He was kidding and yet not kidding.

"Just doing my social research," replied Neal, composing her mouth primly. "Studying rampant consumerism in action."

Father Steve laughed, invited details, and did not seem to disapprove.

"I want to have Kevin over for dinner. Is that okay with you all?" Neal asked a few days later. "Maybe Saturday night?" She was sure he would call her during the week and come in to Chicago for the weekend.

"I won't be here," said Jake. "St. Stephen's is having Grandparents' Night. The choir is going to sing. But that's okay."

"I've got to work," Leo said. "I'm taking over for Andy at the shelter. He has to go to a wedding."

The others didn't say anything.

"I don't want to invite him if two of you aren't here. The point is for him to meet you all."

"Why?" asked C.J.

"Why? Because he's interested in what I'm doing. He's an old friend. Well, never mind. I'll ask him another time, when everybody's going to be home."

"Do you intend to go on dating him?" asked C.J. after a pause.

Neal laughed. "I've had dinner with him once. If I see him again, is that dating him?" Neal softened her tone, reminding herself that they were a community and that she was only one of five. "I have a feeling you're all trying to tell me something. Do you think it's wrong—my going out to dinner once in a while with my old friend?"

The three men looked at Maggie, as though it had been prearranged that she would be their spokesman. "No, not wrong, Neal," Maggie said hesitantly. "But we wonder—I mean, I wonder—well, we're a family sort of. We've committed ourselves to simple living, simple living together. If one of us goes a different route—" She left her condition hanging.

"But I'm not going a different route. I'm committed to simple living just as the rest of you are. Just because I went out on the town one night doesn't mean I've bagged my commitment. Does it?"

"But is it appropriate?" C.J. asked. "Is it consistent for a person pledged to a simple life to go out and spend a couple hundred dollars on an evening's pleasure? It's a matter of integrity."

Neal was determined not to get angry. "Integrity," she repeated reflectively. "I wonder. I am honestly committed, *honestly*, to you all. To our simple life. But we can't control the way other people live. If I hadn't gone to dinner with Kevin, he'd have invited somebody else. He was psyched for a big evening. He probably does that every weekend. That's *his* life." Then she had to smile at her own rationalization. "I enjoyed it though. Yes, I certainly threw myself into it."

"Didn't you even have a twinge?" asked Maggie.

"I don't think so. If I did, I drowned it in another gulp of champagne. Can't you understand, any of you? It just felt so good to forget everything serious and be young and crazy again. Don't you ever get a mad urge to break away? Just for a little while, an evening? Not any of you?" Leo grinned and shrugged; C.J. looked exasperated; Jake smiled meagerly.

"I'd like to break away and fly out to see John," Maggie said sadly. "But I *wouldn't*."

What a load of guilt they were piling on her. Did they mean to do it? And were they justified? A surge of rebellion and resentment was building up inside her, which she made one more effort to master. She answered Maggie with careful calm. "No, you wouldn't, because you'd have to buy a ticket and make a reservation. That would give you time to think. Maybe if somebody handed·you a ticket and said the plane leaves in an hour you'd go. With me it was kind of an impulse thing. Just go out to dinner. I didn't *plan* to carouse like that. I certainly didn't reject my commitment to simple life. I didn't and I don't."

"It's okay, Neal," said Leo. "Hey, let's drop it, you guys. We've beat it to death."

"I probably won't ever do *that* again," Neal assured them. "That's one reason why I want to have Kevin over here. I want him to share how *we* live." She tried for a light note. "It may challenge the materialist in him."

The discussion ended, but a stiffness and coolness remained, Neal thought. She sensed that it was not, after all, the expensive evening that bothered them but the notion of her carrying on a life separate from her sister and brothers.

"We're not nuns and priests," she said to Maggie, when they were lying in their beds that night. "Is there any reason why I shouldn't sometimes see an outside friend?" Maggie sniffled. Was she crying? "Maggie, what's the matter?"

"Oh, nothing." Her voice was thick with suppressed feeling. "Nothing, really. I'm sorry. I just miss John so much. I'm so lonely. It's so hard to be separated." She gave a little sob. "I don't see why we have to be kept apart."

A harsh thought formed in Neal's mind. "Do you mean—" she began. She couldn't complete the question. It seemed so unworthy.

"No, we're not nuns and priests, Neal," Maggie replied. "But we're living that way, sort of. That's the way I see it. Look, Company of Barnabas wouldn't let John and me join the same community. We're in love, going to get married some day. They wouldn't let us be together this year because Barnabas people are supposed to sort of put aside personal commitments for this year. That's the way I look at it."

"And you think that I oughtn't to go out with Kevin because you and John can't be together? But Kevin is just a *friend*."

"He's a boyfriend. Maybe I'm wrong about this. But don't you see my point?"

"I don't think it's the same at all. Kevin is a casual friend. If I never saw him again, it wouldn't matter much. He's not a *personal commitment*."

"But you used to be in love with him."

"No! Oh, I suppose I was kind of in love with him way back then. It was so long ago. I was a different person, a kid. I'm certainly not in love with him now. Or he with me." Maggie sniffled again. "So if I go out with him once in a while, or have him over here, it's not like I'm doing something that you've had to give up. It's entirely different."

"But we're a community. And when you close us out, it hurts us all. Especially Jake."

"What do you mean, especially Jake?"

"Jake cares for you so much. You know that."

"Cares for me!" cried Neal, shocked. "You're crazy. What are you talking about?"

"Oh, I'm sorry, Neal. Maybe I'm wrong. But it seems to me that Jake is always watching you. And listening to you. And wanting to please you. Haven't you noticed it yourself?"

"No way," said Neal flatly. It could not be so. It must not be so. Maggie was simply romanticizing the situation out of her own loneliness. "Because you're in love, you think everybody else is. I assure you, Jake is not in love with me. I am not in love with Kevin. And you're blowing this whole situation all out of proportion."

"I'm sorry, Neal. You're probably right. I'm so self-centered. I was taking such a one-sided view. Oh, Neal, forgive me for criticizing you." Now Maggie was openly weeping. Neal turned on the light and hopped out of bed to sit beside her and smooth her hair, uttering the reassurances that Maggie so often needed: that she was not selfish, that it wasn't wrong of her to give way to loneliness, that it was only natural she should sometimes get discouraged, that they all loved her and sympathized, that she was a wonderful cook and housekeeper, that her school-children were undoubtedly progressing, that above all she had the treasure of her John's love.

They kissed each other goodnight at last. Neal lay in the darkness, wondering grimly whether her two hundred dollar fling had been worth the exhaustion of defending it. She almost hoped that Kevin would never call her again, so that she could avoid any more of these ridiculous arguments and recriminations. She had probably better not go out with him if he did call, and she certainly would not invite him to dinner. But even as she formed this resolution, another voice inside her insisted that she *would* go out with him and *would* invite him to dinner. She was in the right, and her sister and brothers were wrong, and she would make her position prevail.

Friday morning as Neal was hurrying to work at St. Vincent's Center her eye was caught by a huddled figure lying on the wide ledge of a boarded-up delivery platform. The man's back was to the street, his head hunched into the corner of the enclosure, his knees drawn up, his hands out of sight. One of his shoes was missing, and he had no socks. His pants and his tan-and-green plaid jacket had parted in the back, and pale bluish skin showed in the gap. Near his gray foot stood an empty wine bottle.

Neal stared. There was something familiar about the tan-and-green jacket. She couldn't see his face but she knew that this man was a patient at St. Vincent's. Her heart pounded. Was he dead, frozen to death? The temperature was around twenty degrees, and

the wind was cutting. She looked up and down the street for a policeman, but there wasn't one in sight. A businessman hurried along
and Neal looked at him pleadingly but he wouldn't meet her eyes.
She stepped a little closer to the man on the ledge, reluctant to
touch him. "Hey!" she said. Then more loudly, "Mister!" She tried
to remember the name of the man who wore a jacket like this. Fearfully she put her hand on his shoulder and shook it a little, but the
figure remained inert. She shook harder and the man jerked,
straightening his leg just a little. Neal jumped back. He wasn't
dead. A sickening smell came from him. Neal turned and ran
toward the Center.

To her relief she saw Jack Leahy getting out of a car a few yards
from the door. Jack was the Intake Coordinator. This was his business.

"Oh, Jack, come quick. One of our patients is lying in a door
down there. No shoes." The man's name suddenly came to her.
"Charlie Parr. Down there, near the corner, in that boarded-up
doorway." Jack wheeled around and started toward the place, Neal
following a few steps behind. She wished that Jack would tell her
to go back, yet she felt a dreadful obligation to see this through.

Jack shook the man hard, grabbed his arm and tried to haul him
to a sitting position. "Charlie, wake up! Come on, Charlie—up." He
pounded his back, hit him on the legs, seized his hair and pulled.
"Charlie, get up, man." The man jerked, groaned, and curled
tighter, as Neal watched from a few feet away. He could move, he
could groan, he wasn't dead, so why couldn't she leave and let Jack
handle it? She didn't want to look at this. This was a man's job, she
caught herself thinking.

"Come on, Neal, give a hand here," shouted Jack. "We've got
to get him over to Detox. He's almost frozen. Get up, Charlie." He
yanked Charlie's feet off the ledge and half-turned him around.
"Take his arm," he ordered Neal. Jack managed to get hold of the
arm he was lying on, and Neal seized the other, and they pulled the
comatose man to an almost vertical stance. His face was gray except
for the dark crust of blood on one cheekbone. He felt very stiff. He
couldn't balance on his feet; Neal and Jack were holding him up.

Jack yelled in his ear. "Stand up, Charlie. Walk! You're
gonna die if you don't." Charlie's eyes blinked and he made a
momentary effort to support his weight. Jack kept yelling at him,
as he and Neal dragged and carried him inch by inch toward the
corner. The Detoxification Center was around the corner and a

block away. People passing by watched them in curiosity or disgust. "Come on, Charlie, walk!" urged Jack. Charlie growled something unintelligible, but he managed to take a step. Then he slumped and they dragged him. He stumbled a step or two more. They pulled and carried. Neal's arm and back were screaming—she'd never make it.

"Come on, Charlie. Way to go, Charlie," cheered Jack, when he took two steps in a row. "Detox, here we come! Move it, man. Boy, do you stink, Charlie!" he laughed. "Come on, you need a bath. Keep going, that's it. Don't you wanna get out of those pants?"

"I can't do it, Jack," Neal gasped, as Charlie began to sink on her side.

"Come on, we'll change places." Jack grabbed Charlie under both arms and held him up until Neal could get around to the other side. "Keep going. Only half a block. Walk, Charlie, walk!"

Neal scarcely knew how they got the rest of the way. She had shut off every sense against the outrage of sight and smell, and the agony of muscle. She sat on a bench just inside the door of Detox while Jack and an aide lugged Charlie through the entry process. She was shaking violently and fighting a surge of nausea or tears or both. She hoped nobody would look at her or speak to her until she got herself in control. A gaunt black woman filled a styrofoam cup from a coffee urn, and brought it to Neal, and turned away without a word. Her somber silence spoke understanding. Neal sipped at the scalding drink and felt a little calmer.

Jack Leahy came back after fifteen minutes. "Hey, nice going, Neal. We made it. Charlie's gonna be all right. A frostbitten foot, though. How do *you* feel?"

"Shaky," said Neal, trying to sound humorous.

Jack sat beside her on the bench and put his arm around her. "That was rough, kid. I'm sorry you had to do it. I'm used to this stuff, but it's hard on a rookie. Especially a girl. You saved his life, though. He could have died there."

"Well, you too—" gulped Neal. His comforting words made the tears threaten again.

"Yeah, both of us." He stood up and drew her to her feet. "Well, it's all in the day's work, kid. We'd better get back." On the way back to St. Vincent's he kept his arm around her shoulders and didn't say much. As they passed the ledge where they had found Charlie, they saw the wine bottle still standing there. Jack let go of her, seized the bottle, and threw it furiously against

51

the brick wall of the building. "That damn bottle!" he cried. Then he looked with comic remorse at the shattered glass which littered the sidewalk.

"Oh boy, that was a mature thing to do. Look at that." He started picking up glass. Neal helped him gather the pieces and dump them into a sidewalk trash can. When they finished they were almost laughing.

Charlie Parr's relapse was gloomy news at the Center. He had been doing so well. He had been through the first and second phases of treatment and had gotten back his old job in Lester's Cafeteria kitchen. The trouble was that a couple of Charlie's old drinking cronies worked at Lester's. Charlie's counselor had warned him about the temptation that this would be. In fact the counselor had tried hard to get Charlie a different job, but he hadn't been able to turn up anything. He and Charlie had talked it over, and Charlie's AA group had helped him stiffen his resolve not to be led by his old buddies. For two months Charlie had worked and stayed sober, and he had visited the Center several times to show himself off in his new slacks and his tan-and-green plaid jacket. He was very proud of himself.

Too proud. It was an old story. "The recovering alcoholic must never get cocky," Joan Kinsella often said. "You're never cured. You must never underestimate temptation. That devil in the bottle is always there, waiting to pounce on you if you let your guard down."

So Charlie's buddies had no doubt persuaded him that he could have one drink with them for friendship's sake. Just one and then stop. Such things often happened to the Center's patients, both during and after their treatment. The staff members had learned to expect it. They steeled themselves to see former patients drinking from a bottle on a nearby street or in a doorway, but it was always a blow to everybody's morale when it happened.

"Come on, folks, buck up!" Joan urged them. "We've got other people to worry about." She insisted that the staff show a positive, optimistic attitude to all patients, and that this attitude be honestly felt. One of Neal's jobs was to make a weekly poster for the bulletin board showing the small successes that both staff and residents had made: Mrs. Schorski has now been sober for six weeks; Len Grubinski has a part-time job at Benjamin Packing; Janie Rawls passed her first test in bookkeeping—hurray, Janie! One line on the poster always read the same except for the number: Joan Kinsella, sober for five years, seven months, and one week.

The current poster had a line about Charlie Parr: Congrats, Charlie! Two months on the job. Six months sober.

Neal took it down. She always changed the poster on Friday anyway. She sat at a table in the crafts room and began to letter the date across the top of a new poster. Her hands were still shaky, and she spoiled a sheet, and then another sheet.

"You had a baptism of fire today," said Joan, stopping at the door as Neal was cramming the spoiled sheets into the waste can. "You're not a rookie anymore." Though she didn't smile, there was a sort of stern approval in her tone.

"You know what? I wanted to run," Neal confessed, looking her in the eye. "I found out something about myself. I wanted to be protected from that ugly sight. I wanted Jack to shoo me away. No job for a woman—that's what I wanted him to say. Can you believe I still have this inside me? Poor delicate little Cornelia, she can't haul a stinking drunk to Detox. Jack *made* me do it." She laughed wryly. "I'm shocked at myself. I've still got these stereotypes like 'no job for a woman.' "

"It had to be done. You did it. You're learning."

"The hard way," said Neal, turning back to the poster.

Kevin Lindemann called Neal from Vandalia and asked her to go out to dinner on Saturday. "Okay, but listen, Kevin, some cheap dive this time. Remember, I'm living a simple life."

When he came on Saturday Kevin had located a little Mexican restaurant in the far north of the city, "cheaper than McDonald's and more fun." He agreed to take a bus instead of a taxi. So they went, and ate *tostados* and *chile rellenos* at orange plastic tables with noisy Mexican music playing on the jukebox. Patrons were allowed to bring their own wine or beer in from the liquor store nearby.

"I'll get the cheapest bottle of wine they've got," promised Kevin. But Neal insisted on Coke. She kept thinking of the empty bottle standing on a ledge next to the frostbitten foot of Charlie Parr.

On the way back on the bus she told Kevin about Charlie Parr and her work at the Center, and all about her commitment to the Company of Barnabas.

"What does that name mean, anyway?"

"It comes from the Bible. It's a part at the end about the apostles, how they had all their possessions in common. Nobody was in need because everybody shared. A man named Barnabas sold his land and put the money into the kitty. That signifies how we're supposed to live."

Kevin shook his head. "I wonder about that, Neal. I respect what you guys are trying to do, but I don't think you can make a dent in the problem that way. It's so vast—poverty, I mean."

"But that's what people always say to get out of doing anything. They say it about nuclear arms, too. The problem's too big."

"But it *is* too big. I'm not callous, Neal. The other day I saw an old derelict guy going through a trash can. It bothered me. I thought why him and not me? And I gave him five bucks. But he's still poor. I didn't do a thing."

"Yes you did. He had a good meal for a change. That's something."

"Probably he had a bottle of booze."

Knowing what she knew, Neal couldn't contradict this. "Well, anyway, Kevin, you *acted*."

"It was just a gesture. It had no effect at all on the general problem. Or even on *his* problem. It seems like what you do is the same—just a gesture."

"You've got to come to dinner with us," Neal said. "And meet the others. C. J. Bruckberger will explain it better than I can. Bricklayer, we call him, when he's pounding home a point."

"I'd love to come," pressed Kevin. "When?"

Neal hedged a little. "Well, soon! Maybe Thanksgiving. But listen, Kevin, we pray, you know. Are you ready for that? We're a Christian community—reflections, sharing, that sort of thing. Even when we have guests."

Kevin laughed. "Hell, I'm a Christian, Neal. A Notre Dame grad. Have you forgotten?"

So Neal invited him to have Thanksgiving dinner with her sisters and brothers.

7

*M*ost of them worked on Thanksgiving. St. Vincent's Center of course kept open and served a turkey dinner at noon to its residents. Leo was busier than usual at the men's shelter which also served a turkey dinner in three shifts to any man who turned up. Jake's parish choir sang at an eleven o'clock Mass on Thanksgiving, and he was free after that. C.J.'s Neighborhood Association was staging a Thanksgiving Day march downtown and a two-hour demonstration in front of the Garstner Building. This building contained the offices of Planeta Development Company, which was buying up old tenements, evicting the renters, and converting the buildings to condominiums. Planeta had acquired three buildings in the Foster Avenue neighborhood and sent eviction notices to the tenants, and this was the subject of the Neighborhood Association's protest.

Of course on Thanksgiving Day there would be nobody in the Planeta offices, or even in the Garstner Building, but only on a holiday could the Association muster a sizable demonstration. And the downtown streets would be relatively empty, so the marching group would stand out. C.J. had notified all the TV stations and he hoped to get his protest well covered on the evening news.

Jake offered to drive his car down after Mass, park it in a nearby lot, and join the picket line in front of the Garstner Building, but C.J. shook his head. "Naw. Thanks anyway. It might get rough. You could get hurt."

Maggie was in charge of the Thanksgiving dinner, which was going to be chicken fricassee instead of turkey. It was cheaper, and besides they all agreed that Neal and Leo would be revolted at the very sight of turkey after serving dinners all day long. Father Steve Rota came over to join them, and brought a portable television set so they could catch C.J.'s demonstration if it should make the news. When Neal got home from St. Vincent's, Kevin had already arrived, and they were all sitting around watching the six o'clock news.

"Kevin, you're here! I'm sorry—" began Neal.

"Quiet. Here it comes!" cried C.J. But it was a false alarm. The reporter on the screen was not in front of the Garstner Building but at a puppet parade in Oak Park. "There were two different photographers there," C.J. insisted excitedly. He kept changing channels so as not to miss his story.

Neal slipped into a seat on the couch next to Kevin. "Hey, welcome. You met everybody?" she whispered. "I wanted to get here earlier but I—"

"Quiet!" yelled C.J. It was a false alarm on another channel: a heartwarming scene of elderly people filing into a restaurant where the owner was giving free Italian dinners to anyone over seventy.

55

"It's Thanksgiving, C.J." Neal pointed out. "People want to see something *nice*. Not pickets and obscene signs and stuff."

"We didn't have any obscene signs. Hey, this looks like it—damn it, they had the cameras there. Why the hell?" He switched channels furiously.

"Channel 7 was over at the shelter this noon," announced Leo, coming in from the kitchen to set the unmatched glasses on the table. C.J. glared at him. At that very moment a reporter began a syrupy lead: "And there were warm spots all over cold Chicago. . . . " A series of clips began to unroll: Thanksgiving dinners in church basements, school cafeterias, nursing homes, and shelters.

"There's Leo," screamed Maggie. The scene had dissolved almost before she said it, but it had unmistakably been Leo's shelter, and Leo himself in the background bending over a table with a tray.

"Did you see yourself, Leo? That was you, wasn't it? Did you know you were on? Why did they show it so fast?" They were all clamoring and laughing and staring at the set as if they could make it rerun the scene. Then the segment ended and the national news began.

Neal exchanged with Jake a glance of wicked hilarity at C.J.'s discomfiture. But Father Steve clapped him on the shoulder.

"Neal's right. They've got to show human interest stuff on Thanksgiving. Especially at dinner time. You'll be on the eleven o'clock news for sure."

C.J. grumpily assented, they turned off the set, and gathered at the table for their thanksgiving prayers, which Neal hoped Kevin would not find uncomfortable. In fact he already seemed at home with them all. He had dressed tactfully, she noted: his jeans were old, and his gray sweater was unraveling a bit at the wrist. In fact he looked much shabbier than Jake.

He complimented Maggie extravagantly on her fricassee. "Fantastic!" he exclaimed, as she refilled the platter and brought it in. "Neal didn't tell me you ate like this. This is *poverty?*" he helped himself liberally. "I expected bread and water." He drank zestfully from the pickle jar that served as his wine glass. "Fantastic meal!"

But after dinner, off guard perhaps with the wine, he got into an argument with C.J. about the condominium he had bought. It was in a rehabilitated building, not owned by Planeta Development, but doubtless converted in the same kind of unjust manipulation of the poor. C.J. claimed to know the block and the developer.

"Sure, they promised that neighborhood people could buy some of the units. Discounts to people that had lived in the building. What a farce! Did you believe that?"

"I didn't hear it. And didn't care. Listen, I saw an ad. A condo for sale. Convenient location. The price was right. I didn't ask for a history."

"Don't you ever think about what this is doing to families, this development boom? What it's doing to the city, even? It's pushing poor people out of their homes, into the streets. My God, you worry about crime and welfare. What else is there for the poor?"

"Look," said Kevin mildly. "The condo was already finished. I wasn't even the first owner. Whatever the builder had done, it was past. I don't think I'm responsible for the past actions of everybody I buy something from."

C.J. shrugged and shifted to another angle. "It's not even good for uptown Chicago, you know. Uptown used to be a really rich mix of people. Poor and middle-class and upper-class. And different ethnic groups, Indians and Mexicans, and blacks, and Jews. It was a good place to live—not homogenized. Full of variety."

"There are black families on my street," said Kevin. "Mexicans too. A black guy owns the condo next door to mine. Several Jews in the building. It's still a good mix."

"It won't be for long. Developers are driving the poor out, and that means most of the ethnics and most of the families with children. And the old people. Before you know it, Uptown will be nothing but rich singles and couples. No old. No children. Maybe a few rich blacks and Jews, but no Hispanics or Appalachians. You'll all be living in your high-rise boxes, with your doormen to guard you from thieves, and your electronic garages to keep out muggers, and your locks, and your alarms—hell, it's that way now. Towers of wealth, and streets churning with crime and misery." C.J.'s voice got louder and bitterer, and he glared at Kevin as though he held him responsible for it all.

Kevin began to feel the needle. "Hold it a minute. You liberals—" he began.

"Liberals!" hooted C.J. "Here it comes—liberals. Bleeding-heart liberals. Egghead liberals."

"You idealists," said Kevin with deliberate calm. "You idealists are fighting the very thing you want to preserve. The mix. You ought to *welcome* these developers. They're bringing in people with money and style, keeping Uptown from becoming a ghetto. You want a mix—"

"Damn right. How long will it be a mix if—"

"Look at that Lake Beach project. The developer was all set to build in fifty units of subsidized housing. The poor would have been right in there. And he was going to build a supermarket and drug-store, along with the fancy shops. Then one of your tenant groups sabotaged the whole thing. Sued him because he wouldn't build *two hundred* subsidized units."

"Absolutely right. Fifty units for the poor in the middle of five hundred. What a laugh!"

"Man, you're blind to everything but one side. Try for a min-ute, just for a minute, to imagine the other side. Here's a tenant renting an apartment that costs eight hundred a month. Next door to him is a family that pays two hundred and the federal government pays the rest. And what's more, the poor family doesn't know how to take care of the property and the hall's a mess—"

"Oh God, there you go!" shouted C.J. "The vicious stereotype. The poor are dirty. The poor are irresponsible. The poor are slobs and sluts." C.J.'s freckled face was bright pink with anger and frus-tration.

Leo picked up the wine jug and began refilling glasses. "Cool it, Bricklayer," he said mildly to C.J. "Here, drink a little. Gimme your glass, Kevin." And he poured wine into Kevin's pickle jar.

Father Steve began to tell them about a family he knew in a subsidized apartment, and the discussion went on in more con-trolled tones. Neal was disappointed in Kevin for displaying that discreditable narrowness about the poor. Up to that point, she thought, he had been holding his own in the argument with C.J., staying civil and reasonable. His example made sense: certainly most people would object to paying expensive rent if half of their neighbors were getting subsidies for identical apartments. C.J. was too one-sided, too passionate, too over-bearing. She had felt a sneaky satisfaction in seeing Kevin get the better of him. But then Kevin had spoiled it by showing the same old threadbare prejudice against the poor that had infuriated her back at Notre Dame. When he had told her of his compassion at seeing a derelict going through a trash can, she had felt her heart warm toward him. But now here he was showing all the old party-line clichés: the poor are lazy; the

poor have no morals; the poor have limited intelligence. The poor
are poor, and will always be poor, because they are inferior. He
hadn't grown at all. But she felt irrationally disgruntled at C.J. too
for bringing out Kevin's shallowness.

The Thanksgiving dinner, for Neal, was not a success.

Christmas was only weeks away and the question of volunteers
going home for Christmas was becoming thorny. The Company of
Barnabas handbook had a section under "Simple Life-Style" that
addressed the question of Christmas trips. "Volunteers should reflect that Christmas travel, even when paid for by parents, is not an
expression of simple living. Each community should makes its own
decision about Christmas travel, and each volunteer should be willing to act as the community decides." This seemed to mean that all
of them must weigh each one's case, though their service jobs affected the decision too.

Neal's parents had begun pressing her in November. "It
won't be Christmas if you're not here," her mother wrote plaintively. Neal knew it wouldn't. They weren't a big family: besides
Neal there were just her parents and her older brother, Tony.
True, Tony still lived at home, and no doubt the three of them
would try to carry out all the rituals that had grown up among
them since Neal and Tony were children. For instance Neal's
largest present, and Tony's too, always had to be brought in, gor-
geously wrapped, from the front porch on Christmas morning.
There had been a little fiction in the early days that Santa
couldn't get down the chimney with the bicycle or the phono-
graph, and had to leave it on the porch. They kept on doing it
that way. And they had other little customs, as most families do,
about what they ate on Christmas Eve, and what glasses they
drank the Christmas champagne out of, and the wording of their
toasts. Four people can maintain these ceremonies joyfully, Neal
thought, but with one missing there would be something flat and
forced about it all. "Of course we'll send you the plane fare," her
father kept saying. He couldn't see that it would offend against
her pledged poverty. Couldn't the poor accept gifts?

St. Vincent's Center, however, would not close. Christmas
holidays, even more than other holidays, were times of special
stress for alcoholics. These were the days when recovering alcoholics were most likely to lapse. Those who had jobs would have
free days. Lectures and recreational events at the Center were

more important than ever to keep them busy and to keep up their spirits and their resolve. But Joan Kinsella was understanding. "I know how parents can pressure you," she said. "And really, I feel for them too. Do as you think best." It would have been easier if she had said: "We absolutely cannot spare you."

Leo did not even consider going home, and he had managed to reconcile his parents to this from the beginning. The men's shelter, like the Center, would be more urgently needed than ever during the Christmas period. C.J. was not going home, either, even though community organizing would be almost at a standstill. Most people in the neighborhood would have their minds on families and celebrations, and wouldn't come to meetings. But C.J. planned to help Leo at the shelter and give some of the shelter workers time off with their families.

Maggie wanted to go home to Cincinnati, and had the best case: St. Rita's Alternative School would be closed for the holidays. Maggie's father couldn't afford to send her a plane ticket; she would go on the bus, having pinched for three months to eke out the fare from her allowance. John Sims was coming from California to visit *his* parents in Hamilton, less than twenty miles from Cincinnati. His parents had sent him the ticket.

"What about *his* work?" asked C.J. tactlessly. "Isn't prison ministry crucial at Christmas?"

"He's only coming for three days," Maggie explained, her tone anxious and pleading. "John is an only child, and his parents—John says 'How can I be sensitive to the feelings of the outcast and be insensitive to the feelings of my own parents?' "

John's answer helped Jake and Neal. "I've just got to go," Jake said. "Mom worries herself to death about me. You can imagine—" He stopped and shrugged and they were all still. It wasn't hard to imagine the feelings of a mother whose son had to adapt himself to going through life without legs. "I've just got to be with Mom and Dad for a few days. They need it. Need reassurance. I just *can't* refuse them." Jake had worked it all out with Father Corley at St. Stephen's. He would lead the adult choir at Midnight Mass. The children's choir would not sing on Christmas: Father Corley said it was hard to get them together all at one time anyway. Jake would set out right after Mass and drive to Buffalo, arriving in time for Christmas dinner with his parents. There wouldn't be any catechism classes or choir rehearsals at St. Stephen's during that week, and Jake wanted to stay at home until New Year's.

60

The sisters and brothers, in their family council, bowed to the urgency of parents, and Neal, riding on the coattails of Maggie and Jake, called her mother exuberantly: "I'm coming!"

Joan and the other staff members at the Center nodded or grinned understandingly at her decision, but she wished she didn't have to mention her absence to the patients. Janie Rawls gave her a bitter stare when she explained that she must cancel her usual Wednesday counseling session for women job applicants. "My parents are really hyper about Christmas, you know," she said with a deprecating laugh that didn't quite come off. "They'll come up here and hijack me if I don't come."

"Yeah."

Neal thought of Janie's father forbidding her ever to come home again. A wild impulse seized her: Why not take Janie home with her? But Joan would never allow it; she hadn't wanted Neal even to invite Janie to dinner. That would have been offering "a crumb of friendship," she had said. Taking her home for Christmas would be offering a great deal more than a crumb; it would be a massive commitment that Joan ought to respect.

Yes, a massive commitment. Neal saw herself calling up her father and asking for a second airline ticket for "a friend." That would be no problem. But arriving at the airport, her parents waiting, arms outstretched to embrace her and eager to welcome her friend. And then—Janie. She saw Janie through her parents' eyes: the odd, squat figure with the large head, the frowning face—after months of working with her, Neal had almost ceased to think of Janie as ugly and grotesque—the dowdy clothes from Good Will stores. No, she couldn't do that. Even if Joan would permit it, she wasn't strong enough to handle that kind of commitment.

"I'll only be gone a few days," she said lamely to Janie.

"Yeah."

8

"Your hair looks terrible, darling," her mother said on the way home from the airport. "I'll call Spiro first thing tomorrow. He'll fit you in, if I ask. He'll give you a really good cut."

Her parents were having a cocktail party the next evening, Christmas eve. Tony had asked some of his friends, so there would be young people, too. "It's really for *you*," her mother said fondly. "We've invited just a few of our good friends—people we know you like. And a few new ones who want to meet you. And your aunts and uncles of course."

"A cocktail party on Christmas Eve? I didn't know people had cocktail parties on Christmas Eve. Aren't we going to Midnight Mass?"

"Of course. The party'll be over long before that. It's not exactly a cocktail party, anyway. Sort of a tree-trimming party."

"Except that the tree is already trimmed," her father chuckled. "Your mother would never leave that to a bunch of party guests, right, Dot?" It was a family joke, her mother's compulsiveness about tree-trimming. She insisted that each strand of tinsel be separately hung.

"I've kept a few ornaments for the guests to hang—if they want to." Her mother hurried on to the subject of what Neal would wear. "When you go over to Frontenac for your haircut tomorrow, you can drop in at Montaldo's and pick out something smashing."

"I was afraid of this!" moaned her father, slipping with relish into his role. "Neal's home an hour and already the two of you are getting ready to bankrupt me. I'll have to get another mortgage."

It was all very dear and familiar, like her bedroom with its big four-poster and the ruffled canopy. Everything at home looked so clean, so spacious, so voluptuous. Her own bathroom full of thick towels and pink porcelain. Her big closet crowded with clothes she had forgotten. "Look at this," she exclaimed to her mother, rummaging through them. "I don't need to go to Montaldo's. Oh, I love this." She pulled out a green georgette. "I only wore it once." She held it up in front of herself. "I love the color."

"It looks droopy. Smashed in there like that. I think you ought to have something new for our party."

"I'll press it. It's a gorgeous dress." Neal laid it on the bed. "You know, I almost wish we weren't having a party. I thought we'd just have a family Christmas Eve, you and Dad and Tony and I. Oh, I know the party will be fun, but—"

"*Tonight's* our family evening."

The family dinner was roast beef, rare, local news, and teasing, and not too much of Neal's life. She was bursting to talk about her life, and did make some exuberant contrasts between the way she lived in Chicago and the comfort of the O'Connor dining room. "We drink out of peanut butter jars," she said, sipping from her crystal goblet. "We only have one tablecloth—plastic. You wipe it off. We never have roast beef. We hardly even have meat."

"Can you believe it, Dot?" her father marveled. "It wasn't like this when we were supporting her. We had to feed her steak or lobster every night." Her mother hoped she was getting enough protein.

Neal launched into her most absorbing topic, the job at St. Vincent's Center. She told the harsh story of Janie Rawls, her own age, an alcoholic and drug-abuser, repudiated by her family.

"I almost brought her home with me for Christmas."

"Why didn't you?" Her mother's quick sympathy for an outcast spoke. "We would have welcomed her."

"They're not supposed to leave the place until the treatment is finished. I'm counseling her. She's really intelligent."

"Counseling her?" her father asked. "How can you counsel her, Neal? What do you know of such things?"

"I mean job counseling. I'm trying to help her improve her job skills. And I'm counseling her about her addiction, too. I know a lot about alcoholism now. I've gone through the whole program of rehabilitation—just as if I were an alcoholic myself. It's a shattering experience." She started to describe some of the films, and then stopped herself with a laugh. "It's not dinner table talk."

She sensed relief in all three of them. Her father remarked with mild sententiousness that professional training was very important for dealing with social problems. Noble motives, he said, did not guarantee a person the wisdom and expertise to right the wrongs of society, or cure the miseries of individuals. Great harm, he said, could sometimes come from amateurs meddling in people's lives.

"Now, wait a minute," he said, when Neal bristled at the word "amateurs." "I know you're not exactly an amateur, after what you've already seen. But you could be much more valuable as a counselor—or an advocate—if you'd get some training. Psychology, sociology, law—any one of these would make you much more effective."

"But it takes years to get those degrees." Neal thought of Charlie Parr lying on the ledge freezing to death. Neal O'Connor was in law school and did not see him, so nobody pounded him awake and dragged him to Detox.

"You ought to take the long view," her father answered. "That is, if you're really serious about this kind of work, and not just having a do-gooder fling."

"I hate that word 'do-gooder'! It's such a put-down. Don't you think I'm sincere?" demanded Neal.

"Yes, I do. I didn't mean it as a put-down," her father said gently, but Neal was angry.

"How about yourself? You're on the board of Catholic Charities. Would you call yourself a do-gooder?"

"Oh, honey, I'll take back the term if it offends you."

"And I'm not just having a *fling*. I'm not just playing at poverty." Neal remembered Joan Kinsella's irritating phrase. "I'm honestly trying to understand people who are poor and ignorant and powerless."

"I believe you and I respect you for it. What I'm trying to say is that if you continue to be serious about this kind of work—"

"I can't imagine walking away from it."

"Then you ought to think about getting professionally trained. This is a highly technical world. The problems are highly complex. Amateurs and volunteers can't solve them. Am I right, Tony?"

Tony nodded sagely. He was an engineer at IBM. He knew the importance of technology. He pointed out that if Neal wanted to go to graduate school in the fall, she'd have to start applying within a month or two.

"And I'm not just giving you cheap advice," her father added. "I'll support you through a graduate program."

"I'll think about it." Neal couldn't recall that Joan Kinsella had any professional degrees. She had been in the advertising business. Neal opened her mouth to describe this "amateur" who had been rehabilitating drunks for four years, but her mother intervened.

"Let's go and sit by the fire. It's Christmastime, and we want to enjoy it. Tony, you clear these things and I'll bring the coffee. Joe, see if we have enough logs. Neal, you sit, darling, and put your feet up." And thus she recomposed the family group into a harmonious scene, with the Christmas tree lighted, and the presents piled beneath it.

Later Tony asked Neal: "Want to go out to Houlihan's and have a beer?" Of course Neal wanted to. "You'll probably run into some Domers."

Among the wicker and hanging plants of Houlihan's Neal said, "I think I'll have a Coke."

"Have you given up drinking? Is that part of your job?"

"No, I haven't given it up. I just feel like—hey, there's Chris Eberle. And Sheila—" Faces began to come clear as she adjusted to the dim light, and cruising acquaintances from Notre Dame, St. Louis U., Washington U., and Umsal stopped to greet her and Tony. Bar talk and scrappy reminiscence, introductions, shouts of recognition, music. Neal never got around to explaining, to herself or to Tony, why she was drinking Cokes.

"I'll have a ginger ale," she said to the bartender whom Joe O'Connor had hired from the country club to serve at the Christmas Eve party. A ginger ale could pass for a whiskey drink and she didn't have to explain anything.

At first Neal enjoyed the party. The buffet table looked beautiful. A cateress of genius had provided a tableau of food both artistic and luscious, and she unobtrusively repaired the tableau as shrimp were plucked and mushrooms dipped. The Christmas tree and the bowls of live holly and the ropes of evergreen that decorated the rooms asserted their woody fragrance even against the women's perfumes. Neal caught a glimpse of herself in a mirror and knew that the green georgette dress, with its full graceful sleeves, was perfect for a Christmas party, perfect for her own dusky beauty— though she didn't actually permit the word "beauty" into her consciousness. Yes, Spiro had given her a stunning haircut. That morning as he had turned and tilted her head and frowned superciliously, she had stiffened with hostility, remembering Jake's hands combing and cutting and caressing her hair. She always felt exhilarated after one of Jake's cuts. He knew how to suit her face, she insisted to herself, staring coldly into the mirror at Spiro, who was making a little play of repairing a botched job. But afterward she had to admit that Spiro had turned her out charmingly.

Her mother approved. Her aunts gushed. Gallantries poured over her from uncles, family friends, Tony's guests. She was hugged, patted on the cheek and shoulder, kissed, hailed as a beauty and a saint. "Mother Teresa of Chicago," her Uncle Jerry kept booming. "Nealy's going to give me a lock of her hair, aren't you, Nealy? I'm going to keep it for when she's canonized." It was too silly and exaggerated to require more than giggles of protest. Neal didn't mind it.

Later Lyman Briggs, her father's stockbroker, was more offensive. "What's it all about?" he asked, backing her against a cabinet. "A magnificent creature like you, living in a slum, taking care of drunks." His eyes seemed to relish her in a way that was not avuncular; yet she had bounced on his knee in her childhood. "Now tell me, what's the point of it?"

Neal forced a smile and tried to slide away from him. The question was unanswerable in that time and place. He blocked her and took her glass. "Here, you need a fresh one. What's this? Scotch?"

"Ginger ale, please." A chance to escape while he applied to the bartender.

"Now don't go away. Right back. I want to talk to you, young lady." He kept his eye on her while he made his way to the bar, and the room was too crowded for Neal to get far, though she managed to move out from the wall. Soon he was back, handing her a fresh drink and gazing into her face at very close range.

"Mr. Briggs, this is scotch," she protested, making her tone polite. "You didn't—"

"Not Mr. Briggs. Lyman. Scotch, yes. You're not a little kid any more. Drink your scotch, sweetheart, and tell me why a pretty girl—" Somebody jostled him against Neal, and scotch spilled on the green georgette. Lyman Briggs seized a napkin and began dabbing vigorously at her skirt. His face was very red. Neal wondered how many scotches *he* had had.

"That's all right, Mr. Briggs. It will dry. It won't stain." She turned away, set her drink down on a buffet, and plunged through the crowd.

The rooms had gotten very hot, and somebody had opened the front door. Neal stood in the doorway and breathed the cold air. A few snowflakes were falling, she saw. Christmas carols were playing on the stereo, but the party had grown so loud that the music was drowned. She strained to hear, and made out a phrase of "O Little Town of Bethlehem."

She wasn't allowed to stand there very long. She was pulled back and again hugged, flattered, teased, and kissed. Why did older men, even relatives, always want to kiss you on the lips, and so lingeringly? Did they pride themselves on demonstrating that they were still lecherous? she wondered contemptuously. Everybody was looking a little drunk, too; voices were very shrill; conversation was silly and repetitious. Neal was getting heartily sick of jokes about the "angel of the streets" and "Mother Teresa of Chicago." Her smile felt stiff from responding to hackneyed compliments. Then it occurred to her that she was playing the typical non-drinking wet-blanket, censorious of all those who were having fun.

66

"I've left my drink somewhere," she said, wriggling away from an embracing aunt. "Carl, will you get me a scotch," she called to one of Tony's friends who was heading for the bar.

When Carl passed it to her over a couple of heads, she took a big gulp. She needed to get a little buzz on and enter into the spirit of the party. The whiskey sent fingers of warmth all through her, and helped her to listen indulgently to Aunt Beth, who was clinging to her arm and reciting a tale of wrongs. Aunt Beth was her mother's youngest sister; she was married to Uncle Rob, who was always changing jobs; they had five little children. "I'm rich," Beth insisted. "Five children, all bright and adorable. I don't need a mink coat. I don't *want* one." She looked around the room belligerently as though there was a plot to force a mink coat on her. "We can't afford to entertain like this. We can't afford to entertain, period. I almost didn't come tonight. I haven't had a new dress in years. My sisters! With their Anne Kleins and their Nippons—that's a Nippon isn't it?" She eyed Neal's green dress greedily.

"I don't know. I think so."

"They haven't got five children. Not one of them. Sally and Pat, three each. Your mother, only two. Oh, sure you can have new clothes, and minks, and a boat, if you—I tell you, honey, I wouldn't trade my wonderful family for all of their boats and Florida condominiums and swimming pools."

"You're lucky, I guess," said Neal politely. When she had begun talking to Beth there had been several other people in the group, but they had melted away. And who could blame them?

"Lucky?" repeated Beth bitterly. "What choice did I have? It really burns me up. The Church turns around on birth control now. Too bad about Beth, ha-ha. She got caught before the switch. She's got her five to feed and raise. Now you kids can have it your way, live it up, take your time about having children, travel, buy a hundred thousand dollar house. Rob and I have never had a single vacation. We can't even go to a movie. We had our kids, like the Church said—"

"Aunt Beth, I don't think the Church has turned—"

"Sure I'm fat. When you're poor it's easy to be fat." Neal, dizzied by the switch, tried to muster a denial, but before she could utter it she realized that Aunt Beth was, in truth, at least fifty pounds heavier than when she had last seen her. Her creamy oval face was now puffy, and a plump little hand raised the drink to her lips. A very dark drink, Neal noticed. "When you're poor you eat

67

potatoes, and macaroni, and bread. What's more," she added fiercely, "you eat whatever the damn kids leave on their plates. You can't afford to waste it."

"But it's wasted anyway if you don't need it."

"You can talk. Your mother only has two children. It's easy to be thin if you're rolling in money. Sure, eat lamb chops. Eat shrimp. Take a sauna—"

"But, Aunt Beth—"

"Play golf. Play tennis. Who needs tennis? I tell you, I wouldn't change places with them. My children are my wealth. I haven't got a house like this. I've got something better. I've got five beautiful children. A husband who loves me. What have *you* got?" She glared at Neal, pulling her arm away and swaying slightly.

Neal giggled. "I've got a Nippon dress." Then she slipped her arm around the fleshy shoulders, and pressed remorsefully. "Come on, Aunt Beth, let's get some food. There's luscious stuff. Marvelous shrimp. Even caviar, if it's not all gone." Beth let herself be led, partook of shrimp, of caviar, of turkey, of salted almonds, Greek pastry, Sacher torte, and a token carrot stick. Neal held out her drink to be replenished.

The party blared on. At ten o'clock Mrs. Hutchens was pounding out Christmas carols and seven or eight revelers were leaning on the piano and singing what they could remember of the words. The stereo had been silenced. By eleven o'clock the crowd had notably thinned, but those who were left seemed to be digging in for a long stay. Neal's feet hurt. She hadn't worn high heels for months. The cateress and her helper were deftly removing plates and glasses and rearranging the table so that it still seemed to offer plentiful food. The caviar was gone and so was the Greek pastry, but there were platters of turkey and ham, a sliced fruitcake, a cheese tray, and lots of cookies and bonbons. An urn of coffee had appeared. Several guests had taken cups, but the majority were still drinking scotch and bourbon, and the drinks were darker. The conversation was darker, too. There were ugly words about a divorce case, an angry argument about the Middle East, an even angrier one about a football coach, and much talk of money, the stock market, and tax shelters.

"Are you having fun, darling?" Neal's mother asked.

"I guess we aren't going to Midnight Mass."

Her mother glanced around helplessly. "No, it doesn't look that way. Never mind, we'll all go together in the morning."

At a little past midnight Neal slipped away and went up to bed. When she turned the light out she could see that a thick fresh snow was covering the trees and lawn. It looked like Christmas but it didn't feel like it. Was this the family Christmas she had come home for, this noisy celebration of indulgence in food and drink? How shamefully out of key with the humble cave in Bethlehem, she thought angrily. She wished she had stayed in Chicago, and spent Christmas Eve at the Center, perhaps playing cards with some of the residents, or watching *Miracle on 34th Street* with them. She imagined a little scene: Jake had stayed in Chicago too, and he brought his guitar to the Center, and they got all the residents to sing carols and then served them coffee and cookies. Janie was there, and she met Jake, and received an inarticulate message about the transcendance of inner beauty over physical deformity. Neal found herself crying with bitterness, frustration, and a few other confusing emotions, among which was the disagreeable sense that her own behavior had not exactly embodied the spirit of Bethlehem.

Her mother came to kiss her in the morning and bring her a cup of coffee in bed. "Merry Christmas, darling." It was a sparkling sunny day, with five inches of snow, but not cold. Her mother gave her the program of the day: they would eat their traditional Christmas breakfast of waffles and sausages, then they would open their presents, and they'd go to noon Mass together. Dinner that evening would be at Aunt Sally's. "Drink your coffee, and then come down in your robe. Daddy's stirring up the waffle batter now."

Then it seemed Christmasy. Breakfast in the dining room: they always ate it in state on Christmas instead of in the cramped breakfast nook. Almost all traces of last night's party had been cleared away. Only the lace tablecloth and the centerpiece of holly and red roses, and a few silver dishes of nuts and candies on the sideboard remained of it. Tony looked a little pale and hung-over.

"How late did it go on?" Neal asked, pouring syrup over her waffle.

"The last die-hards left about two," her mother sighed.

"*Your* relatives," Joe O'Connor quipped. "The Kremers are all noted for their staying power," he told Neal and Tony.

69

"Why did you go off to bed so early, Neal?" her mother asked. "Everybody was asking where you were."

"Early? It was after midnight. I thought it was a cocktail party."

"You didn't even say goodnight to anybody."

"Should I have? Wouldn't that have been rude? It would make them feel they ought to leave. That's what I thought, anyway."

"It was rather rude for the hostess to go off to bed while the party—"

"Hostess? I wasn't the hostess. And if anybody was rude it was people who are invited to a cocktail party and stay until two in the morning." Neal heard the unseemly shrillness in her own voice.

Her mother rose from the table with ostentatious calm and fetched the coffee pot: "Coffee, darling?" Neal's father sang: " 'Tis the season to be jolly," in his tuneless baritone until they were all forced to laugh and join in.

In haste to change the subject Neal asked: "What's the matter with Aunt Beth? She's gotten so fat."

"She simply eats too much," replied Dot O'Connor, her lips set in a stern line.

"And drinks too much," added Tony.

"You know nothing about it, Tony," snapped his mother. "That's a totally irresponsible remark."

"She says she can't afford anything but spaghetti and bread," Neal went on. "Are they really so hard up?"

"Beth is a spoiled brat. She's always been full of excuses. And self-pity. That's her excuse now: that she's poor. The reason she's fat is that she simply indulges herself. Poor? You should see her grocery bags. Potato chips. Cheetos. Chocolate cookies. Frozen pizzas. She snacks all day long."

"And nips," murmured Tony. His mother glared.

"*When* are we going to have the presents?" demanded Neal, hopping to her feet. This conversation, too, had led into a tangle of hostility.

Neal's big present was, as always, on the front porch, to be hauled in ritually by Tony—too big for Santa to bring down the chimney. In some years a gold bracelet or an airline ticket to Florida had been hidden in a box within boxes, the opening of which produced a roomful of discarded wrapping paper and ribbons. But this time Neal had only to tear the gold paper from one big box to discover what Santa had brought her: a nutria coat.

"Oh, Mom! Oh, Dad! I love it! It's stunning!" She had it on

70

over her robe and was dashing to the mirror to view it. Then she was hugging and kissing her parents, and their faces were bright with joy. At last the room was filled with Christmas happiness, but even in the midst of it, Neal could see another cloud on the horizon. They were so glad she was pleased; they had wanted so much to give her something she would like; they had decided that a fur jacket was a perfect present for *this year*—to keep her warm in that bitter Chicago winter. Neal had grown cagey. She stepped nimbly away from the future and into the immediate present.

"I'll wear it to Mass this morning," she carolled." Oh, what could be more perfect! A white Christmas and a new fur coat. Don't I look smashing?" She preened before the mirror. Then she hugged them again. And then they waded into the rest of the presents.

Kneeling at Mass, enveloped in the velvety warmth of her new coat, Neal thanked God for the presence of mind that had kept her from spoiling the gift for her parents. Of course it was utterly ridiculous to think of taking the coat to Chicago. She almost enjoyed the comic scene: C.J.'s face as she swept into the shabby flat, swathed in fur. After his first incredulity, he would rally. "I get it. Neal's going to raffle it off. For the benefit of St. Vincent's. A dollar a chance, twelve for ten dollars. Oh wait a minute, I'll bet she wants to give it to one of her old bag ladies. Pretty nice for sleeping in a doorway. Might save a life on a zero night."

Her mother and father had bought the coat to keep her warm in Chicago, and she had somehow to break the news to them that it was impossible for her to wear it there. How could they so misunderstand her life and her commitment? But she had to soften her words, avoid the tone of criticism that always seemed to creep into her explanations of the simple life style. She must stop being so self-righteous. She thought with shame and distaste of her comportment at the cocktail party, so intolerant of everyone and everything. Hadn't her attitude been exactly the kind of attitude that had so irritated her in C.J. and Maggie when she had gone out to dinner with Kevin Lindemann? Now the shoe was on the other foot, and Neal O'Connor was acting the chilly, superior censor of other people's morals. How had she fallen into this style? Why should she find fault with a cocktail party on Christmas Eve, with people eating caviar and drinking scotch and paying her compliments and kissing her and enjoying themselves so heartily that they stayed until two? What was wrong with any of that, and where had Neal O'Connor got the nerve to think herself above it? What a pharisee! Wasn't her very posture, head bent over her clasped hands, a mere pose of humble piety? An attitude of setting herself apart from everybody who didn't share her noble ideals?

She jerked her head erect and stared at the altar, trying to follow the Christmas Mass. "A great light has come . . . drenched in the new light . . . amid the splendor of the heavens. . . . " Many phrases about light. Many phrases about the new birth and the new age which was to end man's long slavery to sin. Neal O'Connor felt herself chained in a nasty prison of conceit and self-righteousness. One of the readings said: "Christ's wondrous birth has driven out man's old self." She tried to feel this taking place in herself, a great healing infusion of serenity and humble love entering and pushing out her old self. She caught her mother's eye and flashed her a smile, rubbing her cheek appreciatively against the collar of the new coat.

She thought she had found the right time to speak to her parents about the coat. She had stayed away from the topic all through the afternoon of visitors, and the Christmas dinner at Aunt Sally's, when all the relatives exclaimed over the coat and predicted that the Chicago winter would hold no terrors for a girl so handsomely furred. Only Aunt Beth did not join the complimentary chorus. Neal caught a glimpse of her envious narrowed eyes.

It was the usual Christmas dinner, sacred in its menu and its rituals. The youngest child always said grace, this year Aunt Beth's adorable two-year-old Benjy. The oldest person always received the first slice of turkey, and every year they played the same scenario of trying to get great-aunt Lizzie to admit her age and thus claim her privilege. There was the ritual of someone pretending to serve Grandma Kremer some creamed onions, and she pretending to be horrified at the very smell of them. They always drank a toast to George Bewley, Aunt Lizzie's "beau" of sixty years before, who was held to be still hanging around somewhere, waiting for her to say yes. The children loved the way Aunt Lizzie would smirk and toss her head at this point. They thought Bewley was such a hilarious name. "Boo-ley" cried little Benjy in delight, raising his glass of milk at the toast, and tipping it down the front of his black velvet jacket. Shrieks of hilarity as Benjy and the tablecloth were mopped and dried. "Bewley," the children kept repeating, with explosions of giggles. Even Aunt Beth laughed, and said that nowadays black velvet was drip-dry.

There were presents, mostly funny ones, after dinner, and then carols, and family anecdotes. Then Grandma Kremer and Aunt Lizzie had to be taken home, and the families with young children started gathering snowsuits and boots. Neal and Tony and a couple of their older cousins helped Aunt Sally get the first load into the dishwasher and bring some order into the massive chaos of the kitchen.

Before midnight Joe and Dot O'Connor and Neal and Tony were back at home, sitting before the fire and drinking brandy, with only the Christmas tree lights on, and soft music on the stereo. This was ritual too, cherished ritual. They always said the same things. "It was a lovely Christmas." "It was the nicest Christmas we ever had."

"Do you really like the coat, Neal?" Her mother's question was part of the ritual too. "Do you really like—" and "You can take it back—" were the cues which led to that reassuring chorus that always ended their day: "I love it." "It's perfect!" "It's exactly what I wanted."

Neal cleared her throat softly. "I'm going to leave it here. For when I come home. It's too nice for the kind of life—"

"Leave it here?" Both her parents stared at her.

"It's just too beautiful. I don't want it to get stolen or—"

"But we gave it to you for Chicago. To keep you warm. That's the whole point," her mother protested.

"We'll insure it." That was her father. "You don't have to worry about its being stolen."

Neal emphasized the positive. "I just love it. It's absolutely gorgeous. I'm going to wear it tomorrow to Jenny's brunch." She hopped up and gave each of her parents a kiss.

"But Neal—"

She praised the color and the styling of the coat. She said that a fur coat was a *lasting* gift. For years to come she would luxuriate in this elegant, and so flattering— It was not just for *now*. It was for the future!

"Neal, I just don't understand your attitude." Her mother was almost in tears. "You reject our gifts. Our values. You seem to want to cut us out of your life."

"But, Mommy, I'm not rejecting your gift. I love your gift. I'm crazy about it. But can't you see? This year, in Chicago, I'm living a simple life. I'm not rejecting your values. I'm just exploring some others. I'm not rejecting *anybody's* values."

"You think we spend too much and drink too much. You made that clear to everybody at the party."

"Now, Dot," said Joe O'Connor, patting his wife's arm. "Let's not blow this up. Neal loves her coat, Dot. She's not rejecting her old drunken parents, are you, honey? Why, she loves old drunks, don't you, honey? She's devoting her life to them!" His hearty foolishness went too far, Neal saw: it only exacerbated her mother's hurt.

"Mother, Dad, please." She made a great effort to speak gently. "Please try to understand. Please listen. I've giving a year to living a different kind of life. I've always been privileged. I want to see how it is for people who aren't privileged. There are so many millions of them. Poor people. Outcasts. With no power and no resources. No way of getting justice. Too far gone to be able to climb back. I want to *feel* with these people, not just see them as statistics. They're my sisters and brothers, our sisters and brothers. I want to share their life, at least a little bit. I can't *really* share it. You can't become unprivileged by just moving to the inner city for a year. I still have my education and my good health and my loving parents and comfortable home. I can't disown any of this, even if I wanted to—which I don't. But I want to see the other side—really see it."

"And then what, Neal?" her father asked, serious now. "When the year is up, and you've seen it, what then?"

"I don't know. Maybe I'll just drop it all and walk away. But I doubt that. I hope I'll have some idea of what to do about the things I've seen."

"Don't forget what I said about professional training. You ought to equip yourself as well as you can, if this is going to be your career."

"What I'm afraid of is that I might get caught up in study, in theory, and forget the *people* I've seen. The human beings. The drunk I found in a doorway, almost dead, and dragged to Detox."

"Oh, Neal," wailed her mother. "I can't bear the thought of a girl like you doing such things."

"I'm a woman, Mother."

"On those windy streets, with only a flimsy little down jacket."

They were back to the coat. The coat had come to symbolize

the family affection and standards which Neal was repudiating. How silly it was, Neal thought, shooting Tony a glance of exasperated appeal.

"Neal can't wear her new fur coat while she's hauling drunks out of the gutter," Tony joked. "Down jackets are correct dress for that work."

"There'd be some times she could wear it. You told me you had some dates, Neal. You went to the Drake for dinner."

"Mother, you should see our closet. Maggie and I together have a two-foot space. To cram in a fur coat just for the sake of an occasional date—"

"I'm so disappointed. I thought we had found the perfect present."

There was only one solution, absurd though it was. "I'm taking the coat to Chicago," Neal declared at last.

That concession allowed the curtain to fall on a Christmas scene of family harmony. "After all, you don't have to *wear* the coat," Tony said to Neal privately. That was true, but still she felt frustrated that she had not been able to make her parents understand and accept her life. There was a constant tension, with all of them being very careful not to say anything irritating. Neal kept off the subject of her Chicago life almost entirely when she was with her parents, but to her college friends and to Tony she was expansive about it, maybe even tiresome. She didn't have much interest in anything else, she realized. Big parties with lots of bourbon and pot and loud music seemed boring. "I don't even smoke regular cigarettes anymore," she laughed, refusing pot, and pouring a great deal of 7-Up into a very little bourbon. She kept wondering what they were doing at St. Vincent's Center during Christmas week, and how they would deal with the hazard of New Year's Eve. She worried about Janie Rawls. She missed Maggie, and Leo, and C.J., and Jake.

Three days after Christmas she decided that she had to go back early. New Year's Eve was her excuse. New Year's Eve was the most perilous day of the year for alcoholics, she explained all around, and she must be at the Center to help. So on the 29th of December her parents drove her to the airport. As she went through the door to the ramp she turned toward them and gave a little preening shrug in praise of her nutria coat.

9

C hicago was deep in dirty snow and the cold was brutal. Neal let herself into an empty flat when she got back in the winter dusk. Hurray, she could stuff the fur coat into a plastic bag under her bed before C.J. could see it. The apartment seemed so deserted that she wondered whether C.J. and Leo had left town after all. The kitchen looked as though no meals had been cooked. The coffee pot was disassembled on the counter. C.J.'s bed, however, was tumbled as usual, and his filthy terry-cloth robe was on top of it. Jake's room was neat, as always. But he wouldn't be back until after New Year's. Neither would Maggie.

Neal stowed her coat and unpacked her bag, feeling let-down and forlorn. A homecoming with no one to welcome her. She read the newspaper she had bought at the airport. Would Leo and C.J. come home for supper? Should she try to put a meal together? She checked the refrigerator; it was almost empty. Two eggs, a shriveled apple, a can of Tab, a quarter-loaf of bread. There was a half-gallon container of milk which felt very light when she lifted it out. She sniffed it. Sour. On the pantry shelf there was a can of baked beans, a can of tomatoes, and a box of cornflakes. At the sight of the meager larder, Neal suddenly realized that she was very hungry. Should she go out to the deli? The cold was forbidding. She could wear the fur coat, she decided, tonight when nobody would see it.

She had pulled it out of its plastic bag and was putting it on when she heard the front door open. She shook it off and crammed it clumsily back into the bag.

"Neal?"

It was Jake's voice. She ran into the hall. He was edging his guitar case through the door and dragging a canvas pack behind him.

"Jake!" She bounded forward and took the guitar case from him, then threw her arms around him. "Hey, Happy New Year or something! I didn't think you—"

"I know!" He held her tight, drew back to look at her, laughing at the unexpectedness, then hugged her again. "I came back early. Missed the damn place."

"Me too." She giggled, holding him. It seemed hilarious somehow. "Come on in. Let's close the door. The hall's freezing." She pulled his pack inside. "I'm so glad to see you!" The force of her gladness surprised her.

The heedless questions bubbled between them. When did you get in? How was the trip? Have a good Christmas? How's your family? Where is everybody?

"The place looks abandoned," Neal told him. "There's absolutely nothing to eat. I was just going out to the deli. I'm starving."

"Wait, you don't have to! My car is a traveling deli. Really! My mother has loaded me up with so much stuff—" He was starting for the door, with his stiff gait. "I've got practically half a turkey, part of a ham, cookies like you wouldn't believe, grapefruit."

Neal pulled her coat out again and followed him out to the car. The trunk of the car was crammed with bags and bundles and cake tins, a net bag of grapefruit, and several jugs of wine.

"We don't have to unload it all now," Jake said, as Neal began to balance a cake tin and the grapefruit and a heavy sack. "Wait, that's too much for you. Here, let's just take what we want to eat now. Here's the turkey. Yes, take the cookies. Do you want the grapefruit tonight? The guys can unload the rest when they come back."

The wind froze her ears and neck. It was too cold in the street to be selective. She took the sack and the tin and left the grapefruit. Jake lifted out a jug of wine and a smaller sack and then slammed the trunk. It was hard for him to balance anything heavy, and he had to set down the jug before he got up the two steps to the door. Neal went back for it. Later she made another trip to the traveling deli for additional supplies as they planned their feast.

"I got this coat for Christmas," she said sheepishly.

"It's beautiful. Very becoming."

"I'm afraid to let C.J. see it."

"Why?"

"It's a luxury."

"Not in Chicago."

"All the same." She hid the coat again before they began to prepare their supper. "I wish I knew if Leo and C.J. would be home. We could wait and surprise them with this wonderful meal. I could call the shelter and see if they're there."

Jake shrugged, laying out slices of turkey and cheese, rye bread, Durkee's dressing. His mother had thought of everything. Neal laughed happily as she wiped off the plastic tablecloth and filled the peanut butter jars with wine, remembering the crystal and linen of home. "I can't believe how much I missed this squalor!"

Jake had missed it too. Their stories, which they exchanged as they ate their meal and drank their wine, were surprisingly alike. They had felt the same tension at their homes: the parents resistant and uneasy about the life they were living, feeling somehow betrayed by their children's espousal of "poverty." Jake, too, had been pinned by relatives and friends wanting to know what he was "accomplishing", and what sort of career this was going to "lead to."

"And everybody seemed to be drinking so much," Neal said. "I'm very hyper about drinking since working with alcoholics. I hardly drank anything the whole time I was home. I was a horrible party-pooper," she laughed. "And here I am, guzzling wine without a qualm." She poured some into her jar. "I wonder why it doesn't bother me here? I felt so out of place at home—as if it wasn't home."

"I know. Me too. I was like a transient. My mother almost blew her stack when I said something about 'going home,' meaning *here.*"

"Isn't it weird? I realized how much we really are a family here. I missed you guys."

"I missed *you.*" He wasn't smiling. It wasn't a pleasantry. There was a somber tone in his voice that agitated her.

"Why don't you sing?" she suggested quickly. "Will you? I'll get your guitar. A few carols."

He moved to the sofa, and she brought him the instrument and sat beside him while he stroked chords and tuned it. "What carols do you like?" he asked.

"Little Town of Bethlehem. Do you know that? That's my favorite."

He began to play and sing it. Neal thought of standing in the front door during her parents' party, watching the new snow fall, and hearing from the stereo the same carol wistfully trying to assert its message against the revelry. "The hopes and fears of all the years are met in thee tonight." That was the line that always moved Neal's heart, so mysterious and profound and yet so simple, like the Birth itself.

"Jake, you sing so beautifully," she murmured. "Especially the low tones." He played slow, reflective chords.

"I sang Little Town of Bethlehem at a Christmas concert at Holy Redeemer School when I was eleven years old," he said. "I was a soprano then. Lots of the ladies cried."

"Oh, I can just see you! I'll bet you were adorable. Did you wear a little velvet suit with a lace collar?"

"Neal, I was eleven years old! No, we wore choir robes." He strummed. "My mother wanted to start me on voice lessons then. But my dad said, wait till his voice changes."

"So then?"

"Pretty soon I started croaking. And for a while it looked like Dad was right. Then in a year or so my voice settled and was—well, just like now. Except untrained, of course."

"So then you started lessons? Go on, tell me."

"Yes, I started with a teacher in the music department at Canisius College. He was a priest, a young guy, and he was terrifically psyched about my voice. I was fourteen. He told my parents—well, he predicted very big things. Bigger than I wanted at that time. All I wanted to do was get the leading parts in my high school musicals. And of course I did that as soon as I grew tall enough for the girls. We did *Brigadoon* my junior year. Know that one?" He sang a line: "Come to me, bend to me—"

"Sing it all! I love that song. We had that show at our school."

He sang it all. Then there was the next musical, in his senior year: *Finian's Rainbow*. He sang "Look to the Rainbow" for Neal. Then he had gone on to college at St. Isaac's, which had a superior music department.

"I had a new teacher, a professional singer, who had trained at the Eastman Conservatory. He was much harder on me than Father Mackey had been, and not nearly as complimentary. He didn't talk Metropolitan Opera. But oddly enough, I began to get ambitious myself. I'd press him about opera. He was strong for discipline: scales and vocalizing. He drove me hard, and my voice improved, and he'd come up with a stingy compliment once in a while. He was a very good teacher."

"I sang in college shows, of course. *South Pacific* one year. We even had operas, lighter ones. I sang in *Die Fledermaus* and *The Merry Widow*. For Prince Danilo in *The Merry Widow* I had to learn to waltz. I was pretty good at it, too." He sang "Vilia, oh Vilia, the witch of the wood."

Neal thought of him waltzing in a tailcoat and white gloves, and she felt her insides tighten at the thought of what was coming. He had never talked about his accident, except for a one-sentence summary.

"And then I smashed myself up." He struck two loud discords

79

on his guitar, and then looked up at her piercingly. "Do you want to hear all this?"

"Oh I do. I want you to tell me about it. How did it happen? Were you drunk? Oh, Jake, I hope you weren't drunk."

"I guess I was. It was only beer, but I had a lot. A beach party, a barbecue. We had a keg. You know how those things are. It was late and I guess we were all pretty smashed. But nobody ever thought of not driving. I don't even remember the accident. They reconstructed it later. There was a long downhill road, and it turned, and just where it turned it went under a concrete railroad bridge. I didn't turn enough. Smashed into the concrete."

"You were alone?"

"Thank God! I had already taken my date home. The car was— maybe you even saw the picture? It was so freaky that the picture was printed everywhere. The car was up-ended, standing on the front of the hood with the roof against the bridge. I was pinned in there for maybe an hour. Unconscious though. I didn't know anything until I saw sun coming in a window next morning. Hospital. My mother standing there crying; my father's face all twisted. My mother had to go out of the room while my dad told me. She couldn't bear it. That must have been the worst hour of his life."

"Had they already—?"

"They had already amputated my left leg. They were still hoping to save the right one."

"Oh, Jake."

"I wouldn't believe it. Refused to believe it. Wouldn't listen. Turned my face away and wouldn't speak to anybody: my father, my mother, the doctor. Then they had another operation, and the right leg—part of it—was gone. The doctor said, 'You've still got a knee.' It was the most obscene thing I had ever heard. I tried to spit." He laughed bitterly. "But I couldn't even do that." Jake sat brooding, playing no chords. Neal didn't move.

"I wouldn't eat. I wouldn't talk. I wouldn't look at anybody. My father sat by my bed for hours. I wouldn't speak to him. Right away the doctor started talking about prostheses. I closed my eyes. Closed my mind. Well, it's all sort of a blur now, but I know days went by and I wouldn't cooperate with anything. I thought I should have died in the accident. Why didn't they let me? So they brought me back! That's their problem. They could do what they wanted. I would do *nothing!* My mother would come to feed me because I

80

wouldn't eat. Finally I did eat, but that's all I would do. They had me in bed with a sort of trapeze rigged up above it. I was supposed to exercise. I wouldn't. A biomedical engineer came and poked around my stumps—is this too much for you, Neal?" He had sensed the shudder that she had tried to hide.

"Go on."

"Well, not to be too clinical, the artificial limbs, the prostheses, have to be planned and fitted even before the—before healing."

"That sounds cruel."

"No, it's the best way, because—well, let's not go into that. It wasn't the pain I was rejecting. It was the idea, the whole idea. I didn't want that kind of life. What good would it be to me? Had anybody ever heard of a legless opera singer? People kept coming to me, a priest, a psychotherapist, my friends, my parents, trying to turn my mind around and get me to cooperate. Even my voice teacher came. And I asked him the question: Did you ever hear of a legless opera singer? He told me Sarah Bernhardt had a leg amputated and still acted. Ah, but when? When she was over sixty and world-famous. And one leg, not two. That shut him up. He couldn't honestly claim that a man with no legs could get *started*. And don't forget, I didn't even know if I could learn to use prostheses. They kept telling me I could but I didn't believe it. I didn't want to believe it. The whole idea was repulsive and horrible and I wouldn't have anything to do with it."

"What made you change?"

"Shame. There was a little kid, a little girl called Haley, on the floor with me. About ten years old. She'd had her legs amputated because of cancer. And while I was bawling like a baby, she was already up on her hideous stilts, clacking up and down the hall. She'd come in and show me how they worked. She had already learned—in only a few days—how to control the knee hinge. She kept telling me to hurry up and get mine and then we could have a race. Shame wore me down.

"Well, it took a long time. The fitting, and the skin grafts, and the therapy, and the refitting. Your stumps have to be shaped to fit—well, I won't go into that. But the devices have to be remade as your stumps heal and your body adjusts itself. I was out of college two years, working on the physical adjustment. And the psychological, of course. I never sang a note those two years.

"Why didn't you?"

81

"I was too angry and too bitter. At God. I was throwing my talent back in his face. Isn't that crazy, Neal? To blame God, when I did it to myself?"

Neal couldn't contradict him.

"I was the one who was drunk. Nobody made me drink. I drove the car. Nothing wrong with the car. That was the worst of it: that I had done it to myself. I'd go over those few minutes, or try to. I can't remember them but I keep trying to relive them, go back and change them. Just a fraction of a turn of the wheel, just a little more brake. It's maddening that in just a minute, a meaningless minute, your whole life can be smashed to bits."

"But you still—"

"Why didn't God help me? What would it be to him? It wouldn't have to be a miracle. He could have slowed me down just a little. He controls the movements of the whole cosmos. He could have slowed me."

"Oh why didn't he?" cried Neal passionately.

"I keep asking him that, even now," Jake said soberly. "I know that a man is responsible for his actions. I did this to myself. But so randomly. It wasn't anything I chose or thought about. He could have saved me from myself."

"It's hard to believe in God sometimes," Neal said. "I mean, to believe in his goodness. Things like this—"

"What drives me crazy is that it seems so meaningless. Why? Why did it happen?" He was staring at his legs, that were not legs. "Is it supposed to teach me something? What? Christ, what? What am I supposed to do with this wreck of a life?"

Then he looked at Neal and his tight jaw melted. "Sorry to make such a production." He bent over the guitar and plucked a slow chord. "Most of the time I tell myself there *is* a meaning, and I'll know it someday. I've got to be patient."

"Do you think God really has a plan for each of us? All worked out and everything? And we have to find the key?"

"Not exactly. I think it's more—sort of existential. Things happen to us. Not that he makes them happen. He likes to see what we'll do with them. Like my accident. Not that it was part of a plan and I have to find the key. But that I have to put meaning into it. It will mean what I make it mean. I don't know what that will be. I'm searching. This year with Company of Barnabas is part of my search."

His parents had opposed his joining the Barnabas volunteers,

82

he said. They wanted him to go to graduate school in music, continue his voice training. They insisted he could still be a professional singer, on the concert stage if not in opera. He could certainly teach.

"But really, they want to protect me. Keep me in an academic atmosphere, with not too many stresses. Close to home, if possible. They're terribly worried about this life. Inner-city, they keep calling it. They're terrified I'll be mugged or something. But I've got to try this. I want to test myself against 'real people.' Like this old battle-ax, Father Corley, and the parish choir, and the children. See if I can make them respect me. Music education attracts me. I like training the choirs. But before I decide to go in for teaching, I have to be sure I can make students respect me. When you're handicapped, some people almost count you out as a man. C.J. does."

"Oh no." Neal uttered her protest before she had time for second thoughts.

"Sure he does. He can't help it. He's such a macho guy. Remember when he was having the protest march and I offered to march with them? 'You might get hurt.' That was his answer. I hate condescension. I hate pity. I'm still a man, Neal."

There was an urgency here that Neal didn't want to examine, a message that she didn't want to receive. "Hey, look at the time! We'd better clean up here. I'll carry out and you can wash." She breezily held out her hand to help him pull himself up, but he didn't take it. He sat there looking at her steadily.

"Do you think you could ever love me, Neal?"

Neal felt her face getting hot and her breath struggling. "What a question! I love you now."

"That's not what I mean. Sure, we're brothers and sisters. I mean—you know what I mean, Neal. Could you?"

Neal fumbled with the dishes from their meal, stacking them clumsily, hastily. "Jake, we're not even supposed to think of stuff like that. That's off limits. Barnabas volunteers are *only* brothers and sisters. We agreed to that." She took a load of dishes to the kitchen. Her hands were shaking. She heard the metallic meshing of his knee hinge which meant he was pulling himself erect. She went back to help him.

"Look at the time!" she said again. It was after midnight. "I guess Leo and Old Macho aren't coming home. Here, I'll carry those. You can wash."

She bustled noisily, scraping plates and putting food away and bagging garbage, while Jake ran hot water into the dishpan.

"I was talking about someday, Neal," he said after a silence. Neal was stuffing a wine bottle into the garbage bag. "I wonder if you find me —" Jake paused, plunging a jar repeatedly into his hot suds—"if you find me repulsive."

"Repulsive? Oh Jake."

"Because of being mutilated."

She pulled herself together and faced him. "Jake, that's a horrible thing to say. Or even to think. I can't believe you asked me that. Don't spoil this evening. I love the way you shared your life with me tonight. It was beautiful." She repeated it. "Beautiful! Now let's finish up here and get to bed. We have to work tomorrow."

Neal wiped off the plastic tablecloth, and Jake poured hot water over the dishes in the drainer and scoured the sink in his usual meticulous fashion. "You can have the bathroom first," he said, squeezing his sponge dry. "Take all the time you want. I'll read for a while."

"What are you reading?"

"St. Augustine," he surprisingly answered. As she stood at the kitchen door, waiting to turn out the light, he laid his hand on her cheek, smoothing her eyebrow with his thumb. "Good night, Neal."

She still felt this ambiguous touch as she showered, undressing in her cold room. It was a brotherly caress, she assured herself, minutes later, as she stood under the lukewarm shower, trying to recall Tony's brotherly marks of affection. She and Jake and all the Barnabas volunteers had pledged themselves to live as brothers and sisters, and her reply to Jake had been exactly right, she insisted. They mustn't even consider any other relationship. By the time she had toweled herself dry and jumped into her flannel nightgown, she managed to place Jake's question firmly into a file marked "Irrelevant."

"I'm finished," she called to him through his closed door.

The wind rattled the windows. The heat had gone down long ago and the apartment was freezing. Neal put Maggie's blanket on top of her own. Finally she remembered the fur coat under her bed. With that on top of the blankets, she began to feel warm and drowsy. Jake was in the shower and the sound of the water was soothing: this was home. She slept.

Some time later she awoke, too warm. Suddenly she remembered C.J.'s question to Jake last summer: What if the place catches fire some night? How long does it take you to get hitched up? And then his solution: Leo and I can carry you out. A cutting example of the very condescension Jake hated. But tonight, with C.J. and Leo away—Neal sniffed frantically. Smoke? If there was a fire she'd have to rush to Jake. She'd have to see him stripped of his dignity, of the manly image he was so anxious to maintain. She'd have to see those "stumps"—horrible word—and help with shaking fingers to fit the gruesome devices which she could not even bring herself to envision.

She jumped out of bed, sniffing wildly. Out in the dark living room, she sniffed. She padded to the kitchen and checked all the gas jets on the stove. Nothing. The place was bitterly cold. It was the fur coat, probably, that had made her feel so warm. She climbed back into bed, casting it off. And finally, after a long time, she fell asleep.

10

*E*verybody at St. Vincent's Center was glad to see Neal back early. The bitter weather was keeping the residents, most of them, from taking the outdoor walks which were encouraged, and the atmosphere was bored and restless. The Christmas season was exceptionally tense for alcoholics, anyway. The television ads were full of family gatherings and presents and parties. Festive twelve-packs were brought into kitchens, and foaming golden liquid poured into tall glasses, with appropriate sound effects. In other ads celebrants toasted the season with wine; everywhere glasses gleamed and ice-cubes tinkled. Residents of St. Vincent's watched these scenes glumly. "I'll have a scotch on the rocks," muttered Tom Scanlon, as a lively office party, advertising snack crackers, interrupted a rerun of "Miracle on 34th Street." Neal heard him but pretended not to. Janie Rawls, who was also watching the movie, frowned indignantly. Residents were not supposed to refer to alcohol favorably under any circumstances.

"I'm glad you're back," Joan Kinsella said. "We really need you. Our residents are stir-crazy. Just a fresh face helps them."

"Are we doing anything for them on New Year's Eve?"

Nothing was planned. Joan herself would be taking the night

off, something she seldom did. Morrie Shipley, her assistant, would be on duty, but none of the other staff would be there. It was very hard to put on any kind of party for the residents anyway, Joan said. They were such a mixed bunch of people, all ages, varied levels of intelligence and education, different backgrounds. What kind of game or activity could they all enjoy together? Bingo was out—that was gambling.

"I could get Jake Traherne to bring his guitar over and sing for them. And get them to sing." She hadn't broached this to Jake but she knew he would do it. "We could have coffee and cookies, and maybe some paper hats, for New Year's Eve."

"I don't know, Neal." Joan hesitated.

"And I could run off some song sheets on the ditto machine. Christmas carols and old favorites. Jake's really good at getting people to sing. It would raise their spirits. Everybody looks so gloomy."

Joan began to favor the suggestion. "If you're willing to handle it. Yes, it might be a good idea. Don't let it get too elaborate. And not too long. An hour or so." She gave Neal some petty cash to buy cookies or doughnuts, and paper hats and horns. Neal set about making a poster to announce the party to the residents. She called Jake at the apartment to get his consent. Yes, of course he would do it. They were having a Watch Night Service at St. Stephen's and the pastor wanted Jake to lead the choir, now that he was back. But this wouldn't start until eleven. The St. Vincent's party would begin at eight.

Leo and C.J. showed up for dinner that evening. They had been living at the men's shelter so that Andy Ragatz, the director, could have a few days off with his family. When Neal came home C.J. was enthusiastically slicing ham from Jake's hoard, eating the scraps that fell off as he sliced. Leo was making sandwiches, with rather meager fillings. Leo still wished them all to eat less meat.

"Put some ham in there, man," C.J. urged. "We've got plenty. We don't want to waste it."

"Ham keeps," Leo commented mildly. But he piled it on more generously.

"Now a couple slices of turkey on top of the ham," said C.J., turning to the turkey carcass. "Jake's Mom sent us a real feast." Leo refused to have turkey added to his ham sandwich, but Neal and Jake applauded the voluptuous sandwiches C.J. was turning out.

"We'll eat tuna fish and spaghetti like always, when this runs out," Neal told Leo. "But when God pours gifts down on us, let's enjoy."

Leo made up on cookies for his refusal of turkey. He told funny stories of the men's shelter at night. "I tell you, being a dorm counselor for a bunch of guys in their sixties and seventies is something else. One old guy got in with a bottle. I don't know how he did it. We practically strip-search them. And then he spilled some of it. No kidding, he was down on his knees beside the bed, trying to lick it up off the vinyl pad."

C.J. had stories too. They were all merry together. Jake and Neal told of their Christmas trips, and their presents. Bold, after a glass of wine, Neal brought out the nutria coat, and tried it on for them.

"Very nice. Looks warm," C.J. said.

"It's becoming," said Leo.

"I was afraid you might think it's a luxury," she said to C.J.

"Not here. Half the women in Chicago are wearing them. Wieboldt's must be selling thousands every day."

"Not like this!" Neal was half angry, half amused. "This is a *real* fur coat. Not a Wieboldt's fake."

"Is real warmer?" C.J. asked.

Catching Jake's eye, Neal burst out laughing. What a deflation! All the fuss she had made about the coat to her parents, based mostly on C.J.'s anticipated disapproval, had been utterly silly.

"What's the joke?" C.J. looked from her to Jake, who was laughing too.

"Nothing! Nothing!" giggled Neal, grabbing the coat to take it back to her room. "I just made an ass of myself again." She wouldn't explain any further, and C.J. didn't pursue it. He was preoccupied with a FANA meeting he was planning for the next week, and the announcement he was going to compose and hand-deliver to every building in the neighborhood. After they had finished eating, he went to the old typewriter which sat permanently, like a sixth place setting, at one end of their dining table, and began to hammer out his copy.

Neal and Jake went over his song-books and selected carols and old favorites they thought everybody would know, for Neal to ditto next day for the party. Jake would sing a few songs first by himself. People were usually slow to warm up, he warned, and it would be a mistake to expect them to join right in. He'd move to something very familiar and catchy, perhaps "Shine on, Harvest Moon," and then Neal was to begin humming and singing a few of the words. The others would take it up, and at that point, when they were beginning to *want* to sing, she was to pass out the song sheets. "Nobody likes to be manipulated," Jake said. "Giving out song sheets right away is like forcing them to participate. You want to give them out just when people are wishing they could remember the words."

It was a grim-looking crowd, Neal thought, looking over the assemblage in the crafts room. They had decided to have the party in the crafts room rather than in the recreation room so as not to interfere with those who preferred to watch television. This was another of Jake's suggestions not to be manipulative. "A party's not a party if you *have* to go to it." And in fact a few die-hard watchers showed no interest in leaving the television set. Janie Rawls sat in a corner of the recreation room, not even looking at television; she was reading one of her Harlequin romances.

After Neal introduced him, Jake lowered himself into the armchair she had arranged for him, and began to strum softly, smiling slightly at one or the other of the audience. His smile did not ask for any responding smile; it simply moved meditatively from one to another. He began to play and sing "Comin' through the Rye." Watching their impassive faces, Neal wondered whether he could ever get them to participate. They were so used to television, which flashed and clattered and sang and chortled all day long before their inert gaze, that they had probably lost all sense of the human performer. Jake sang "For Me and My Gal" and "June Is Bustin' Out All Over," and still as far as Neal could see there was no warming trend. He switched the mood and sang "My Way." Nothing. He sang "I'm a Yankee Doodle Dandy," and at the end of that a voice suddenly called out for "Bicycle Built for Two." Luckily they had it on the song sheet. As Jake began to play it, he signaled Neal to begin humming. Soon other hums started up, and phrases, and the tapping of feet. Neal distributed the song-sheets and the sing-along was in full swing. The television watchers began to straggle in, all except Janie. When they got to "Old MacDonald Had a Farm," Neal gave out the paper hats and put one on herself. The glum faces no longer looked glum; nearly everybody was singing lustily, and there were calls for repeats of certain favorites. It looked as though the party was a success. If only Janie would come and join in. But Neal did not go to urge her, bearing in mind what Jake had said about manipulating.

Instead she plugged in the coffee urn, and began to arrange the cookies and candy canes on the refreshment table. Grace Forrester sidled up to her, smirking.

"Is he your boyfriend?" she asked, nodding toward Jake.

"No, he's my—my brother."

"Oh boy! Your brother!"

"Not my blood brother. We live in a community together. You know, sort of a religious community. In that sense, he's my brother."

"Not your boyfriend?"

"No."

"Good!" Grace leered. "There's a chance for me."

Neal laughed mechanically. It was a joke. Grace Forrester was over forty, probably fifty. But soon she was easing her way over toward Jake, and next she was sitting on the arm of his chair, and next she had her hand on his shoulder and her foot kicking in time to the beat as she sang along with "Harvest Moon."

"Go for it, Gracie," yelled Bill Dorgan raucously from the back of the room.

Neal caught Jake's eye and could hardly keep from exploding at the comedy. But she was nervous, too. This was the kind of thing St. Vincent's Center frowned on, and Neal knew she oughtn't to let it escalate. She looked around for Morrie Shipley, who was on duty in the house, but he was nowhere to be seen. She couldn't embarrass Grace in front of the whole room by calling her to order. Then Jake solved it.

"Now, friends, I think it's time for some music of the season," he said. "Some Christmas carols. Let's all settle down and be quietly grateful for the birth of Christ. Thanks for joining in, ma'am," he said to Grace Forrester with his blessing smile, at the same time indicating to her that she should move from his chair to one of the empty seats. "Now let's sing 'Silent Night' together."

Grace moved. Far from feeling rebuffed, she glanced around with great satisfaction, as though she had been singled out for a decoration. Jake strummed the opening chords and nodded for them to begin. Everybody knew that carol.

Jake and Neal had agreed that after about an hour he would play the final carol, "O Come, All Ye Faithful," and then he would play "Auld Lang Syne," and the singing would end. Of course they would clamor for more, he predicted, but it would be right to end before they got bored. Neal would then serve the re-

89

freshments. They did clamor for more, but Jake was gracefully adamant. He promised to come again soon. He put his guitar in its case, got awkwardly to his feet, and came over to the refreshment table.

"I haven't had so much fun for a long time," said Betty Grubb.

"You sing very good, young fellow," said Paddy McGlynn.

"And you're mighty cute!" cried Grace Forrester, edging her way up to him. Jake nodded his thanks to them all.

The cookies disappeared swiftly, and bearing in mind Joan's advice not to let the party go on too long, Neal gathered up paper plates and napkins, and unplugged the urn. Then she and Jake prepared to leave. But it was hard to break away. "Don't go yet." "Sing some more." The pleas were poignant. When she and Jake left, Neal saw, the party would be over and these sad people in their incongruous paper hats would slump down in front of the television set or play desultory games of cards to pass another few hours of their harsh lives.

"Happy New Year, Charlie. Happy New Year, Paddy. Happy New Year, Grace." Neal went around saluting each one by name, putting as much heartiness and encouragement as she could into the phrase. She stuck her head into the recreation room where Janie still sat in her corner, having ignored the refreshments as well as the singing. "Happy New Year, Janie."

Janie looked up with a scowl. "Okay," she mumbled.

Blaze Curry grabbed Neal's coat as she began to put it on. "Allow me, beautiful lady," he cried, parodying gallantry. He held it for her, and then folded it around her. "You don't have to go yet," he murmured, parodying lechery. "Get rid of him. Stay with me, baby."

"Don't be a clown, Blaze," laughed Neal, shaking him off. You couldn't dignify this with a serious reproof.

"I'm jealous," said Blaze, folding his arms and glaring ferociously at Jake.

Neal shook her head, still laughing. "Happy New Year, Blaze." Then she and Jake slipped out the door.

When Neal reported to Joan Kinsella the following Monday about the party, she described the incident with Grace Forrester. Joan approved of the way Jake had handled it, but she faulted Neal for not stopping Grace immediately.

"Embarrass her in front of everybody?"

"Neal, haven't you learned? You've got to be tough. You mustn't let them con you. Alcoholics are very good at conning people. There are always some who want to bend the rules or beat the system. Be tough with them. They have to learn to live with rules. That's part of their recovery. An important part. Don't protect them from embarrassment. Don't save their feelings. Too many people in their lives have been trying to protect them."

"At first I thought Grace was kidding. I mean, she's old enough to be Jake's mother."

"Even if she was kidding, she knows the rules here. They all know the rules. No sexual talk. No sexual jokes. No sexual gestures, kidding or otherwise. It was bad for all the residents to see her get by with that. You think I make too much of this, Neal, but, believe me, it's necessary. Sexual tension could be explosive in a place like this." Neal decided to say nothing about Blaze Curry's teasing remarks.

"Part of Grace's trouble," Joan went on meditatively, "maybe the heart of her drinking problem, is that her mother brought her up to believe that a girl's only proper goal in life is to get married. Everything was clothes, and makeup, and pleasing men, and being popular. Grace thinks she's worthless because she has no man."

"But she has a profession. Isn't she a teacher?"

"She was a teacher, a grade school teacher, but her heart wasn't in it. It was supposed to be a temporary career, until she got a husband. She was a party girl, loved to go out and drink and dance. If she didn't have a date, she'd call up somebody. She'd pay. She's told me all this. She sees it as being 'liberated.' But between the lines I can see that she always came on pretty strong. Maybe she scared men off. Anyway, as she got older she got more desperate, more aggressive. She'd go to bars and pick up people, take them home. And she drank more and more, and of course didn't get to school, and lost her job. Then got another, and lost that. She wrecked her car. Her mother wouldn't pay her bills any more. Her brother helped her for a while and then he too made an ultimatum. Finally she fell off a porch when she was drunk and broke her leg and was laid up in the hospital. This gave her a period of forced sobriety, and she pulled herself together. She and her mother made a truce, and her mother took her back home on condition that she would never take another drink. She stuck with it for a year. But she couldn't get a job. She had a terrible reputation in the school system by this time.

Her mother has enough money to support her, but life at home was stultifying. And she still had no husband and no boyfriend, and on top of that she's now over forty. No way to meet men except in bars—or so she saw it. She began sneaking out. Well, you can see the pattern. It started all over again. Her mother threw her out, her brother rescued her, then he threw her out. Now neither her mother nor her brother will give her a cent of money until she's been sober for five years, and can prove it. Imagine that! So Grace has got to stick it out here and get over her disease, and get a job, and support herself. You've got to find her a job, Neal."

"A teaching job?"

"No, probably not a teaching job. I don't think she can get a teaching job, with her past. But she's a college graduate."

"What about her other problem? Her man problem? Does she recognize it?" Neal imagined Grace in an office, hanging over men's desks, making advances, losing her job after a wife complained.

"I've talked to her about it. She seems to understand herself a little better than she used to. But then this incident the other night—it makes me wonder."

"Do you think she's a nymphomaniac?"

"No, I doubt it. I don't think it's sex she wants, exactly. It's the status of having someone. She feels that a single woman is simply a cipher. You've got to admit that our society promotes that notion."

"God, yes!" cried Neal. "And we've got to turn that around."

That very day Neal got a demonstration of what Joan meant about being tough. They walked out of the building together, Joan on her way to a meeting at the Detoxification Center and Neal to visit the U.S. Employment Service. Sidling toward them on the street was a former resident, Randy Colson, who had fallen back into drinking.

"Joan. Joan," he called piteously to her closed face. "Stop a minute. Talk to me." He was drunk and filthy.

"I won't talk to you when you're like this," Joan said coldly. "Get sober and then we'll talk." She walked on.

"Joan, please." He stumbled after them, but Joan did not look back.

"That may seem cruel," she said to Neal half a block later, "but it's the only way. To coddle an alcoholic is the real cruelty. *I* know."

11

Neal was trying to find jobs for Janie Rawls and Grace Forrester. Both of them were in Phase II of their treatment: they had fully acknowledged that they had the disease of alcoholism, that they would never be free of it, that they must never take a drink again under any circumstances. They were resolved on this. They were ready to take cautious steps into independence. Janie had become a competent typist and had nearly completed her bookkeeping course. Mr. Ferguson was very much impressed with her. She had outdistanced other students who had started the course ahead of her. He had already offered to send her out on employment interviews, but Janie held back, insisting that she wanted to perfect herself. She was scared, Neal saw.

Each week Neal spent an hour counseling her, trying to show her how to put her best foot forward in a job interview. It seemed impossible that Janie would smile or look pleasant or respond to any civilities about the weather. If only she could be persuaded to improve her appearance a little. St. Vincent's Center had a storeroom of clothes, both men's and women's, that people had donated. Neal went through it, with Janie standing stolidly by, and picked out a white blouse that looked as if it would fit. It was bedraggled from hanging, but otherwise in good repair. "You can wash and iron it and make it crisp," Neal told Janie. "It would be a good thing to wear for an interview. A white blouse is always flattering to a woman."

Janie rolled her eyes contemptuously, but she took the blouse. Seeing her examine the iron as though she had never handled one, Grace Forrester took the blouse in hand and spruced it up for her.

"That skirt's too long," Grace said to Janie. "If you shorten it, you'll look taller. Here, I'll pin it up and you'll see."

Grace had a good sense of style and grooming. She could go into the storeroom and haul out a limp garment and turn it into an outfit for herself that looked almost smart. There was no doubt that *she'd* make a good impression in an employment interview. Neal decided to slip in a tactful caution to her that, after she got a job, she should be discreetly friendly with her co-workers but never flirtatious.

"People sometimes misunderstand," Neal faltered. "Like that night when Jake—I mean, some men would take that the wrong way."

Grace waved it aside. "I was just kidding with him. That didn't mean anything."

"That's what I'm saying. You're naturally friendly. But if you kid like that in an office—" Neal felt the disadvantage of her youth in trying to advise a middle-aged woman on behavior. "All the success manuals say that women in business should be friendly but *reserved*."

"What about men in business?"

"The same, of course."

"That's a laugh. Men can do anything they want. Chase you around the desk. Smack your fanny. Make remarks. I say what's fun for the goose is fun for the gander. Or is it the other way around?"

"But it doesn't work that way," said Neal. "It ought to, but it doesn't. Women still have to play by men's rules." Neal hated to hear herself advocating an unfair accommodation. But the big priority right now was for Grace to get a job and keep it, even under the conditions that resulted from the fact that most offices were run by men. "Maybe you can get a job under a woman manager," she added, brightening.

"God forbid!" exclaimed Grace. "Nothing doing! I want a job where there are some *men!* Where there's some fun! Some life!" She raised her arms, snapped her fingers, and threw a modified bump-and-grind.

Neal re-enacted the scene for her roommates that night at dinner, exaggerating the bump-and-grind a little. "It's funny," she acknowledged, when they all laughed. "But it's also frustrating. Grace calls herself liberated. But actually she's totally imprisoned. She doesn't think she's alive unless she can get some man to play up to her. And she's nearly fifty years old."

"Do you think sex is just for the young and beautiful, Neal?" asked C.J. sardonically.

"No, of course not," answered Neal, momentarily confused. "Anyway, that's not the point. The point is that Grace's life has been bent out of shape by society's view of women. She was brought up

94

to believe that women's lives depend on men. See, she thinks if she gets a job in an office full of women, there won't be any life there. She's a perfect example of how society has victimized women."

"The main thing is for her to get a job, right?" asked C.J.

"Yes, and keep it. If she starts making passes—"

"You're taking this too seriously, Neal. People in offices are always kidding around. It doesn't mean anything. She won't get fired for a little jiggling."

C.J. was probably right, Neal thought. She was borrowing trouble. Help Grace get a job—that was the main business at hand. Grace had surely enough experience and knowledge of herself by now to hold onto a job once she had got one. She had been in the pit of degradation and had come back. She had even kept her sense of fun. How marvelous it was, really, that after all Grace had been through she still had so much zest. Wouldn't she actually be an asset to her future office, bringing an occasional burst of high spirits into the tedium of work? How much pleasanter it might be to have Grace for a co-worker than Janie Rawls, grumpy, truculent Janie, who probably wouldn't even say good morning.

"Janie is another example of the way our society victimizes women," Neal went on. "She has absolutely no self-esteem. None. Why? Because of her looks. American society demands that women be attractive. Janie is very smart. She's a whiz in bookkeeping. But she considers herself worthless. Her whole experience, at college, at home with her family, has convinced her that she ought to crawl into a hole and hide her ugly face. I think it's a crime, a dreadful crime, that our society puts so much value on looks."

"I agree with you." Maggie spoke bitterly. "And especially on women's looks. You guys can't really appreciate what it feels like to be looked over, sized up, rated—and then discarded."

"I know what it feels like, Maggie," said Leo. "I've been there. In high school I couldn't get any girl to go to the senior prom with me. I called up ten at least."

"I even had a blind date walk out on me," C.J. boasted. "A guy fixed me up. When I called for her at her dorm, she took one look at me and broke out in hives. She had to go to the infirmary."

"Oh, you guys!" Neal dismissed their stories. "You've had a few little rejections, but not enough to really damage your self-image, because you live in a world that constantly reinforces you. To be male is to be in command. These women have been permanently warped by the idea that the female must please the male. But we're going to turn this around," she predicted. "*We're* going to do the proposing, we women. We're going to do the choosing and the rejecting. You guys can sit at the telephone waiting for *us* to call."

"We already do, Neal," Leo said. "I've been waiting all my life for somebody like you to call."

Jake stared at her somberly. "You can't really understand Grace Forrester's life, Neal. Or Janie Rawls'. You don't know what it is to be rejected."

"I do. I know all about rejection." Even as she made the claim, Neal felt ashamed of the minor disappointments which were all the evidence she could muster. She hadn't been chosen to solo at the ballet recital. She hadn't made the first-string soccer team. What ridiculous examples! She knew rejection mostly from the experiences of her friends, and even they were trifling and transient experiences compared to the humiliations of Janie Rawls. "Well, all right," she conceded. "I haven't got much *personal* experience of being rejected. But I can try to understand it, can't I?"

"It's the old story," C.J. said. "We middle-class people, educated and all, we can't really, fully empathize with the destitute and unempowered. We can try. We've got to try. But we can never fully do it."

The volunteers often talked about this: that they couldn't cast aside their privileged backgrounds, their good educations, their self-confidence, their good health. They were living in a shabby flat, getting along on a meager stipend, perhaps even more meager than the wages and welfare payments of their poor neighbors. They were supposed to be sharing the life of the poor. Yet they ate wholesome food, and the flat was orderly and cheerful, and though their budget was very lean toward the end of each month, they did enough planning so that they were always able to muster up some sort of meal. In the flats around them television sets blared, junk food abounded, fights were common, family life was disorderly and incoherent. Mrs. Holbrook's son was in jail for knifing a schoolmate; Ellie Johnson had three children and no husband; the Riveras had six children in three rooms, and ran out of food the last week of every month. These people's lives were so full of crises and emergencies that there never seemed to be time for them to sit down and figure out how to improve things.

The volunteers helped them. Maggie often went over to visit the Riveras after she got home from school. She was trying to show Mrs. Rivera how to feed her children more healthily on less money, introducing her to tuna fish and spaghetti and oatmeal. C.J. got a lawyer for the Holbrook boy, and helped other neighbors with their food stamp applications. But what the volunteers couldn't do, they acknowledged to one another in frustration, was truly understand the poor. The more they saw, the more they realized that poverty had a thousand facets and no core.

Neal read the help-wanted ads every day in the *Chicago Tribune* to get ideas for jobs, if not actual jobs, for Janie and Grace and her other clients. The U.S. Employment Office, which she visited regularly, always had some jobs listed, especially for waitresses, dishwashers, and office-cleaners, but Neal felt sure there were other possibilities. "Bowling center manager," she read one day in the *Tribune*. "Night position. Send resume to—" Another ad called for "Guy/Gal Friday. Small construction company needs responsible person to learn all phases of office procedure. Some bookkeeping. Send resume." Could Grace Forrester be a bowling center manager? Could Janie be a Gal Friday?

That nasty little phrase "send resume" was a hazard. A typed resume must reveal those unaccountable gaps in the applicant's past. Neal preferred ads that gave a telephone number, inviting a personal interview. It would be easier for Grace Forrester in a face-to-face interview to slide over those years of being out of work, those jobs lost because of drink. Nobody, including Joan Kinsella herself, had ever formulated any absolute wisdom on whether a job applicant should tell her potential employer about her alcoholism. Each job-seeker had to make the decision. In one case that everyone talked about, a man had impulsively blurted out the facts of his past, after being determined not to, and this had gotten him the job. The employer was himself a recovering alcoholic, it turned out.

But probably in most cases the applicant would lose the job if she revealed that she was in an alcoholic treatment program. There was the matter of the applicant's address, too. That would be a giveaway. Grace Forrester had decided to give her mother's address when she applied for jobs, and her mother had agreed to take messages. Janie Rawls, when she went on referrals from Mr. Ferguson, would give Ferguson Business College as her address. This might or might not hold up with employers. If they asked her for a home address, she would say that she was in the process of locating an apartment.

"How about working for a textbook publisher?" Neal asked

Grace Forrester. That morning she had noticed that Rayburn Publishing Company was advertising for employees in several categories: clerk-typists, copy-editors, and development editors. A development editor, the ad said, should have experience in elementary teaching. "You've been a teacher," she said excitedly to Grace. "You've got a degree in education." The salary was very good, perhaps far more than a person out of work for years could expect. It made Grace uneasy. "But what about one of the other Rayburn jobs?" Neal urged—"clerk-typist even." If Grace could get into textbook publishing, though at a low level, her teaching experience might help her move up.

"I'm no hot-shot typist," Grace demurred. She almost seemed to prefer the job as bowling center manager.

"But that would be a dead-end. In the publishing company you could move up, maybe become an editor." Neal imagined the temptations of the bowling center. There was probably a bar connected with it. "And think of the noise. Wouldn't that drive you crazy? And working at night—"

"I wouldn't mind working at night. I like to sleep late."

"There'd be a lot of people drinking."

Grace shrugged. "Wherever I go there will be people drinking. I've got to live with that. And I will. Don't worry about me. I'm never going to take another drink in my life."

They worked on two resumes, one slanted toward the textbook publishing firm and one toward "managerial" duties for the bowling center, and sent them in.

Janie, dressed in her white blouse and her newly shortened dark skirt, prepared to interview for a job with a hardware company, referred by Mr. Ferguson. Neal went over the probable scenario with her, playing the role of the employer, trying out questions on Janie.

"Are you a good typist?"

"I type fifty words a minute and I'm very accurate." Mr. Ferguson had certified to the employer that she was.

"Have you had any experience at bookkeeping?"

"No, I haven't," Janie was supposed to answer in a confident tone, "but I've finished my course with the highest grade in the class. I'm sure I can learn your system quickly."

"What have you been doing since you left college?"

"I've done some traveling, and taken various courses." Neal

was trying to get Janie to utter this ambiguous sentence with an ingratiating smile, as though acknowledging her aimless immaturity. Then she was to turn serious: "But I've grown up a lot lately, and I'm determined to settle down and work hard."

Neal saw how Janie's hands shook as she got ready to go, and her own heart beat harder with anxiety about the interview. "I'll say a prayer for you," she promised.

She said several prayers. In fact, she had a hard time focusing her attention on anything else that morning. She was running a film about the dangers of social drinking, and after that she would lead a discussion on the subject. While the film rolled, her mind kept straying to Janie, instead of devising questions to get the discussion started. In the afternoon Neal went out to call on Office Temporaries, and when she got back, Janie had still not returned. How could a single interview take so long? Was this a good omen? Perhaps she had been hired and put to work immediately. But wouldn't Janie call up and report this good news? Or perhaps the employer had wanted her to talk to other people in the company. Late in the afternoon Neal called up Mr. Ferguson to see if he had had any news of the outcome. He hadn't. Neal lingered past five o'clock, when she usually left the Center, reorganizing the employment file.

"I hate to leave before Janie comes back," she explained to Joan Kinsella's questioning look. "I want to know what happened."

"You'd better go," Joan said. "It's almost dark, and it's starting to snow."

"Don't you think it's strange she isn't back yet? And didn't call?"

"You'll find out tomorrow. Better go home now." Joan looked weary and grave, and did not attempt to put an optimistic interpretation on Janie's absence. Neal's anxiety deepened. Perhaps Janie's courage had failed her and she had not even reported for the interview. Or perhaps she had been turned down, had been plunged into depression, and had turned to her old solace, the sherry bottle. Neal, waiting on a windy corner for the bus, wet snow blowing into her face, imagined Janie sitting in a dingy bar trying to numb her humiliation. She had a wild notion of trying to trace her to the office where the interview had taken place—she remembered the address on West Madison—and searching the streets and bars in the neighborhood. If only she could rescue her before she had gone too far.

Then the bus lurched to the curb through the snow, and Neal got on. She rebuked herself for her agitation. She was letting her fantasies run wild. And even if they were to prove real, she would have to accept the facts with calm forbearance. The lapse of an alcoholic was not a rare event at St. Vincent's. Blaze Curry had recently dropped out of the Center and had been seen drunk on the street. And there was Charlie Parr, whom Neal had hauled to Detox—but Charlie was back and was trying again. Bessie Chambers had disappeared. These things happened, and workers at the Center had to accept them with equanimity, not allowing them to dampen the positive attitude of their enterprise.

And of course that crazy impulse to search for Janie and "rescue" her was completely contrary to the Center's philosophy. You couldn't rescue people by pulling them away from bars or emptying their bottles into the sink. There was no salvation except in their own will and resolution.

When Neal got home there was another crisis to take her mind off Janie. C.J. had been arrested and was threatened with a night in jail if bail could not be arranged. Leo had gone over to the Foster Avenue Neighborhood Association to try to get the hundred dollars. It was on FANA's behalf that C.J. had got into trouble. The Association had been trying to buy a burned-out building in the neighborhood, which it intended to rehabilitate into flats for low-income people, with an office and hall for itself in the basement. But a condominium developer claimed to have concluded a contract for the building, and now the "exploiter" had wheeled up his machinery and his workers for the gutting of the structure. FANA insisted that its bid had been elbowed aside by political shenanigans. C.J. and a group of protesters had that day linked arms and formed a chain around the whole building, refusing to let the laborers inside.

The police had been called and had ordered FANA to desist. The protesters subsided—they had not intended to offer any violent resistance—except for C.J., whose temper had flared. He had abused the police because of what he called their "contempt" for the rights of citizens. The argument had escalated until he had been hustled into a police car, charged with causing a disturbance and resisting arrest.

Jake had tried to get Father Corley to put up the bail money, but the incident had infuriated the priest and he refused. In fact he had announced that he would no longer let the Foster Avenue Neighborhood Association use St. Stephen's Hall for its meetings.

St. Stephen's would not be associated with lawbreakers and police-baiters.

"I'm on the side of the police," he had told Jake angrily. "I *need* the police. The people of St. Stephen's need the police." As far as he was concerned, C.J. Bruckberger could stay in jail for a week. It would do him good.

The FANA people put up bail, but they were down on C.J. too. The "stop-line" had been his idea and he had assured everyone that it would be peaceful and good-humored. The Neighborhood Association didn't want to get the reputation of being disruptive. It had to get along with the police, too, and with merchants and residents. And now that Father Corley had been alienated, it had no meeting place.

C.J. got home about nine, ranting against the police and against FANA's timid and unimaginative policies. Luckily, however, there had been a reporter at the police station, covering the beat in bored fashion, and C.J. had given him an earful. C.J. hoped to see something in the *Sun-Times* the next day that would call attention to the greedy developer and the crooked politics which favored him.

"When do we eat? I'm starved." He was obviously exhilarated by his exploit.

When Neal arrived at the Center next morning she learned that Janie was back. She had come in very late, and Jack Leahy, who had been on duty, had unlocked the door and let her in.

"Was she—all right?" asked Neal fearfully. Jack would have had to turn her away if she had been drunk. That was a rule.

"She looked sober. I didn't go into it. She was soaked with snow and half frozen."

Later Janie sat stiffly in a chair next to Neal's desk, and without meeting her eyes told the short tale of the interview.

"I went to the office. There was this receptionist. She was expecting me. She told me to sit down. She called Mr. Bradley. He came out of his office. Big smile. He looked at me. Then he stopped, like he remembered something. Went back into his office. Nothing happened for a few minutes. The switchboard buzzed, and she talked in a kind of whisper. Then she called me and said she had made a mistake. The job was already filled."

Neal didn't speak. She was trying to master the fury that threatened to explode from her. Some faint instinct told her that it

101

would be better for Janie if she could make light of the incident, shrug it off—so what? all in the game, that's the way the ball bounces.

"Where did you go?" she asked, after a minute. "I was so worried about you."

"I walked."

"All afternoon? All evening?"

"I walked to Evanston."

"In the snow? To Evanston?"

"Walked and hitchhiked."

"Did you drink?"

"No. I was heading for Flo's Place. You know, a bar I used to go to. All the time I was walking and hitchhiking I was thinking of it. When I got there it was closed. Boarded up."

"Oh Janie, thank God."

"So I turned around and started back. On the bus."

"Did you get anything to eat?"

"I couldn't eat."

Neal felt her eyes smart. She wanted to weep or to scream her anger or to throw her arms around Janie's stolid form and comfort her. She would call Mr. Ferguson and vent her indignation. She would notify the Employment Service of the outrage. She would call the American Civil Liberties Union. She would help Janie file suit. But some little breath of pragmatism blew through her mind, perhaps originating in C.J.'s conflict of the day before, cautioning her to hold her fire. Justice had been violated and the unjust man deserved to be exposed and punished. But would that get Janie a job? Would it soothe her humiliation to have attention called to it?

"You'd better rest up today," she temporized, making her tone very matter-of-fact. "You must be exhausted. I'll see Mr. Ferguson this afternoon and find out what other job calls he's had. In fact, I saw something in the Trib this morning." It was an ad for a receptionist in an osteopath's office. She rustled through the columns and found it. "Must be good typist. Some bookkeeping."

"A receptionist? You've got to be kidding!" cried Janie, her voice cracking.

Neal folded the paper without argument. "Well, we'll find something." She intended to put every ounce of her energy into the search. "The best thing of all," she said, trying to get Janie to meet her eye and accept her congratulations, "is that you didn't drink. That's a real victory."

102

Janie responded with a grimace.

Mr. Ferguson sat impassive in his office that afternoon when Neal described the shameful treatment Janie had received at Bradley Hardware. "He didn't even speak to her! Just looked at her and rejected her. And then made his secretary lie that the job was filled."

Mr. Ferguson didn't seem shocked at the lie. In fact he had already sent another girl over to be interviewed for the job. His business was to find work for his graduates, not to argue with potential employers about their hiring practices. "If he doesn't like her looks, he doesn't have to take her."

"But don't you think it was vile, the way he treated her? Inhuman?"

Mr. Ferguson wouldn't commit himself. "It's up to him," he said, his face hardening. Neal saw that she must not alienate him. Janie needed Mr. Ferguson. And he had been a friend to St. Vincent's, giving free tuition to several residents and helping them find jobs.

She put Bradley's villainy behind her. "So much for that. Do you have anything else for Janie?"

"Not at the moment. But let her come on over and start the advanced bookkeeping course. And practice her typing. She should keep up her skills. Something else will come along."

At home that evening Neal let out her fury and frustration about the incident. She was sure it was unlawful to do what Mr. Bradley had done, to discriminate against a person in hiring because of physical appearance. "It's the same thing as discriminating because of skin color. Or because of a physical handicap." Neal hadn't yet ruled out appealing to ACLU or some other agency to see if Janie's civil rights had been violated. But there was the vexing question whether Janie's interests would be served by stirring up an investigation. "But I just hate to let him get by with that! It's like sitting still and letting evil triumph."

"Social action is like politics," C.J. said sententiously. "Sometimes you have to compromise. You have to let evil triumph when fighting it means screwing up the good you're trying to do somewhere else. You'd better cool it, Neal."

His condescending tone infuriated her. "You're a great one to talk," she jeered. "I can't believe you're lecturing me after your stunt yesterday. You screwed things up for FANA so they don't even have a place to meet. Why didn't *you* cool it?"

He grinned. "I'm learning. I had to crawl to Father Corley today. Beg him to let us use the hall. Promise to never do stuff like that anymore. He gave me hell for half an hour and I had to stand there with my head down and say Yes, Father, Yes, Father, Yes, Father. He told me: 'Get this, Bruckberger. I *need* the police. The people of St. Stephen's need the police. We need them a hell of a lot more than we need you. Or FANA. Got that, Bruckberger?' Yes, Father. You're right, Father. I understand, Father. Please may I kiss the hem of your garment, Father?" They chuckled at the idea of C.J. abasing himself so uncharacteristically. "See, Neal, I speak from experience."

To complete C.J.'s mortification, the *Sun-Times* had not published a line about the incident.

Grace Forrester was turned down for the job as bowling center manager because she didn't have any managerial experience. But a couple of days later she interviewed with the Rayburn Publishing Company and got a job as an assistant editor. The salary was better than she had expected, and she was already talking about getting an apartment and buying new clothes. Neal tried to slow her down, even while pouring out congratulations. Residents were supposed to stay at the Center for a month or so after getting a job, receiving moral support in the adjustment to the life of work. Most residents wanted to do this; they were shaky about taking the first steps to independence. They were supposed to pay the Center fifty dollars a week toward their board and treatment, and to make a firm connection with an Alcoholics Anonymous group. Grace had not done this yet.

"Don't forget, you're an alcoholic," Joan Kinsella said to her sternly. "You have a disease. You're not cured. You'll never be cured. You've got a job, and that's great, but you're still an alcoholic. Don't get cocky. That could be your downfall. You must join an AA group, and be there every week. And you must stay at the Center for at least a month."

When Joan said "You must," few people could contradict her.

Janie went on an interview for a job at a printing company: "Typist, 60 wds min. Gen. office duties." Neal had found it in the *Tribune*. Janie had to take a typing test, and in her nervousness she failed it.

104

"Next time will be easier," Neal assured her, hoping it was true. "The more you interview, the less nervous you'll be."

Then Mr. Ferguson sent her out on an interview for a clerk-typist, but it turned out that the clerk-typist was also to be a receptionist and run a switchboard. Had Miss Rawls ever run a switchboard? No, but she could learn. Sorry, we prefer someone with switchboard experience.

"It was no use arguing," Janie said. "I'll never get a job as a receptionist."

Neal continued to comb the want-ads every day.

One day in February Joan called Neal into her office and offered her a staff job at St. Vincent's beginning in July, when her volunteer year would be over. The Center was going to expand. There was a part of the third floor now unused which could provide an additional twenty beds. A Chicago manufacturing association had given a grant to the Center which would enable it to add to its facilities.

"Of course we can't pay you what you could get somewhere else. But the need is terrific. And you've done so well here."

The offer, and the compliment, took Neal by surprise. "I have?"

"Your initiative in finding jobs. Grace Forrester's job, for instance. Your rapport with the women. Really excellent."

"I haven't found Janie a job yet." Neal's mind was turning dizzily. She had applied to Washington University Law School, having weighed her father's advice to get professional training.

"I don't expect you to answer right now," Joan said. "I'm sure you have lots of other possibilities. I'm almost ashamed to tell you the salary. I wouldn't even have the nerve to ask you except that we need you so much. I've watched you, and I've seen that you really care about these women you're working with. You've put your heart into it. It's really satisfying work, isn't it? When you're answering human needs, money doesn't—" She stopped and shook her head. "I can only speak for myself, though. And of course I have a special stake in this. I don't want to talk you into anything. Don't answer now. Think about it a while."

"I was planning to go to law school," said Neal weakly.

"Jack Leahy was planning to go to law school. That was three years ago. He's still with us. And Morrie Shipley—no, I mustn't try to talk you into it. Just think about it for a while."

105

The proposal both pleased Neal and disturbed her. She was gratified, extremely gratified, to be praised for her "initiative" and her "rapport with the women." She felt mature and successful, and she wished her father could know that her counseling of these women alcoholics had been called "excellent." She remembered how nettled she had been at his contemptuous question: "What do you know about counseling, Neal?"

But to settle in and take a job at St. Vincent's, to make a career of this? To put law school aside and live on a mean salary in a shabby apartment which would be all she could afford, and try to find all her satisfaction in serving "urgent human needs"? It was all right for Jack Leahy, she thought. Jack Leahy was married. He and his wife had apparently agreed to give their lives to urgent human needs. His wife was a nurse and she worked in a clinic for the indigent elderly, and they lived a life of vegetarianism and frugality. But they had each other. It would be a lot different doing something like that, Neal thought, if you had a loving partner to share the commitment. She had sometimes thought enviously of Maggie and John Sims and their future.

Her own commitment had been for a year. It didn't seem fair that because she had done a good job, she was being pressed to extend it. There were all her Notre Dame classmates who had not even dreamed of giving a year of service, who were happily climbing the corporate ladder, pulling down big salaries, flashing their credit cards in expensive restaurants, flying to the Costa del Sol for vacations. They hadn't given anything, so nobody was bothering them. Why should Neal O'Connor, who was already a year behind on the success track, be asked to give more? "How much is enough?" she demanded resentfully of some formless petitioner—Joan Kinsella, or society, or perhaps Christ.

She decided not to tell her roommates about Joan's proposal until she had had time to ponder it. She thought she knew what they would say, and she didn't want to hear it.

12

The bitter cold continued. March came in like a lion. The Chicago sidewalks were black and lumpy with ice; the wind blew as cruelly as it had in January; the only change was that the afternoons were longer. Neal felt no more guilt about her fur coat; she clutched it around her and was grateful. At night, when the heat in the flat went down, she often threw it over her bed to keep her feet warm.

The five volunteers sometimes found their sense of family unity strained. Or perhaps, Neal thought, they were actually becoming *more* of a family, less on guard with one another. The frustrations of their work sometimes broke out in sharp retorts and nagging digs.

Maggie, especially, was under stress in her job. When she had come back after Christmas she had expected that Cleon Jefferson, the wild incoherent child who caused chaos in her classroom, would have been removed to the psychiatric center where he had been certified as belonging. But he was still at school, wilder than ever. The principal, Sister Florence, told Maggie that he was on a waiting list for the psychiatric center but nobody knew how soon there would be a place for him.

Maggie often came home in tears, with stories of children biting each other, cutting each other's clothes with scissors, screaming in the halls, and throwing food in the lunchroom. The weather was so cold that they couldn't play outside for more than a few minutes, and their conflicts mounted because of being kept indoors.

The roommates grew weary of trying to prop up Maggie's spirits, and Neal almost felt relief when C.J. spoke sharply to her. "All right, Mag. Stop whining. You're not the only one with troubles." Then Maggie broke out in apologies which were harder to take than her tears. "Forgive me, all of you, for being so self-centered. I'm so ashamed of being such a drag. I drag you all down. Please forgive me."

Leo was the only one who never lost patience. He would hug Maggie, and pat her shoulder, and insist that she wasn't a drag. He'd praise her cooking and her housekeeping and remind her that they'd be living like slobs if it weren't for her care. When they prayed together, Leo always thanked God for Maggie's care of them, and for Jake's music, and for Neal's sense of humor. Then he would usually make some joke to God about C.J. "Thanks for giving us this pain in the neck. He'll drive us to sainthood." C.J. would nod in a self-satisfied way at Leo's denigration, a tribute to his toughness. He didn't need to be patted and praised as the rest of them did.

Leo urged them to pray together more often. They needed

107

more patience, more understanding, more wisdom to know how to deal with their jobs and with each other, he said. His constant prayer, when they sat around the table together with bowed heads, was, "Lord, lead me to a building we can rent. A landlord who will talk to me." The men's shelter had had one reprieve, but now it was again perilously close to the end of its lease, and Leo was fine-combing the neighborhood for a new location. Everywhere he went he found faces closed against his offers.

Neal prayed: "Lord, help Janie find a job." Janie had been to five or six interviews, and all had been failures for one reason or another. Her bitter experience at Bradley Hardware had not been repeated, but Janie lived through it again at every turn-down. She was convinced that her ugliness was the reason for every rejection, and this conviction made her more mean-looking and withdrawn than she had ever been. Neal was terribly afraid she would drop out of the Center in despair if she didn't get a job soon.

Jake was having physical trouble. He had fallen on the ice and wrenched his knee—his one knee. It was swollen and sore and he had to use his elbow canes to get around. This didn't slow him down particularly, for he was very nimble on the canes. But it worked against his self-esteem. He felt he had less control of the children's choir and received less respect from the adult choir when he was seen as a "cripple." Even Father Corley, he thought, had less respect for him, always suggesting that Jake cancel evening choir rehearsals because they might be too hard on him. "He's kind of writing off the adult choir," Jake brooded, "at least for this year. He's just waiting till my year is up. He used to talk about starting a guitar Mass for the teenagers. He never mentions that anymore."

"That conservative old bastard never intended to have a guitar Mass," C.J. said. "He'd rather bring back Latin."

"Does he ever suggest that you stay on?" Neal asked. "I mean, as regular parish staff?" She wondered whether anyone besides herself had been offered a regular job.

"No. It's cheaper to get another volunteer each year."

"He can't build up much of a choir that way, with no continuity."

"He doesn't care about a choir. My job's a Mickey Mouse job." Jake spoke bitterly. "Not like your jobs, where you're doing things for people really in need."

"I don't think it's Mickey Mouse to bring some beauty into people's lives," Neal countered hotly. "People need music in their lives. In their worship. You've done a lot for St. Stephen's." Jake shook his head gloomily. "You'll be off the crutches soon," she added.

"Canes. These are canes," he snapped.

"Excuse *me*."

"I hate the word crutches." His scowl melted into a self-mocking grin. "Isn't that silly? As if crutches could make me more of a cripple than canes. I'm sorry I jumped on you, Neal."

"It's okay. I understand."

C.J. was frankly looking forward to the end of his year with FANA. He was going to Georgetown Law School. He had always realized, he said, that to effectively "empower the unempowered" he needed a mastery of law and economics. Too many of the people in FANA were simply earnest amateurs. "I've learned a lot this year," he conceded, wincing at the thought of some of his lessons, "and I'll learn plenty more before the year is over. About the problems of the unempowered. And some of the stupidities of neighborhood politics."

His boss at Foster Avenue Neighborhood Association had been severe on C.J. since the police-baiting incident. He told C.J. to shave off his straggly beard and spruce up. FANA didn't want to be seen in the community as a group of kooks and radicals. The Association needed the respect of the churches, the landlords, the merchants, the tenants. C.J. had grudgingly shaved the beard, and had bought a couple of decent shirts at the Good Will store, but his appearance was still scruffy.

"Aren't you going to shave today?" Neal needled him one morning at breakfast, looking away from his fingernails. "Your beard has better than a three-day stubble."

"I can't get into the damn bathroom! That guy takes half the morning." Jake was in the shower with the bathroom door locked. Originally he had always taken his shower at night when there was less traffic, but sometimes of late he had let it go until morning. It irritated C.J. that Jake had to have the bathroom to himself. "Why can't I shave while he showers?" he complained. "I'm not going to look at his damn legs. I'm not curious. Why does he have to—"

"Let's not talk about it. Can't you shave at the sink?"

Leo had hung a mirror over the kitchen sink to provide another shaving and tooth-brushing station.

109

"I need the bathroom for other things besides shaving," answered C.J. grimly.

Yes, they were like a family, bitching over trifles.

Then Maggie lost her job. Sister Florence told her that she didn't have the temperament for teaching children with behavior problems. She couldn't establish the firm authority that such children needed, and they were actually deteriorating instead of improving in her classroom. Sister Florence was kind and sympathetic. She praised Maggie's dedication and assured her that she would easily find a more appropriate way to use her skill and energy.

Maggie was devastated. She wanted to leave Chicago at once, go home to her father's house, or go to San Francisco to be near John—but she didn't have the money for that. They all argued against her leaving. To break up their community before their year was over would be a failure for all of them.

"We're a family," they all told her in different ways. "You don't leave your family when you have some bad luck. That's when your family means most to you."

But she protested that she wouldn't be contributing anything. She would get no more stipend from her school. Their skimpy funds would be depleted by one-fifth. She'd be living off the rest of them.

"Maggie, you contribute more than any of us," C.J. said, and the assurance meant more because it came from him. "We can make it without your salary. But not without *you*."

Jake reminded her that their jobs, all their jobs, were of secondary importance in their volunteer year. The *community life* was the major thing. "You've lost your job, but you haven't lost your sisters and brothers."

"Don't go away from us, Maggie," Neal pleaded.

"Don't go away," they all pleaded.

"But what will I do all day?"

They reminded her of their neighbors: the Riveras, and the Holbrooks, and other people in the building and on the block. Maggie had already done a lot in helping these mothers to shop and cook wisely, but they needed steady reinforcement. It would be a full-time occupation, said C.J., just to respond to all the crises and daily inadequacies in these troubled homes.

"But that's not a job!" Maggie wailed. "I'm supposed to have a job."

110

They summoned Father Steve to help them persuade her. He spoke of the future.

"When you and John are married and are teaching somewhere in Latin America, you'll have setbacks, just as here. Setbacks and failures are part of everyone's life. You won't leave John. He won't leave you. You'll carry him or he'll carry you. Let your community carry you now. They want to, and it's *right*."

They pleaded with her in many other versions of these words, and finally overcame her reluctance.

Only a week later they were pleading with Leo in the same way.

It was a bitterly cold night toward the end of March. A frigid wind seemed determined to sweep Chicago into the Lake. It was slicing through the cracks in the windows of their flat. Even C.J., who usually went barefoot indoors, was wearing shoes and socks against the cold. He was typing furiously at the table, writing a petition that FANA was going to present to a paper company which had let out two dozen laborers without notice. Maggie was mending clothes for some of Mrs. Rivera's children. Neal had the eleven o'clock news on the radio. Jake had already gone to bed.

Leo came in, ushering a filthy, ragged derelict, obviously drunk, who slumped down on the floor with a toothless grin on his face.

"Can Jonesy rest here for a while and get warm?" Leo asked, glancing around at the three of them without really meeting their eyes.

C.J., preoccupied, frowned and nodded and went on typing. Maggie stared in alarm at Jonesy, and then at C.J., obviously expecting him to take action.

"It's below zero outside," Leo said with a weak little grin. "Jonesy's trying to find a place to stay tonight. He needs to warm up for a little." Jonesy sniffled.

"If I'd known we were having company I'd have made some munchies," Neal said. Comedy seemed the only way to keep disgust at bay. Already the relative warmth of the room was beginning to penetrate Jonesy's clothes and unseal his terrible odor. Maggie clutched her sewing, fled to her bedroom, and slammed the door.

"He can't stay at the shelter," Leo explained to Neal, who was the only one listening. "The rule is, if you're drunk you can't come in. And you're drunk, aren't you, Jonesy?" Jonesy's eyes were closed. He was now quite limp. Leo went on in a roundabout way, talking about the rule, which he approved of, that nobody could come into the men's shelter if he was drunk or if he had a bottle or weapon with him. Anybody, drunk or sober, could get a cup of soup and a sandwich out of a window next to the entrance, but to come in and eat sitting down, or to stay overnight—no, not unless he was sober. Neal knew all this, but Leo went on explaining it, perhaps to gain time for Jonesy. Drunks meant trouble in the dormitory, Leo said; they caused fights, they got sick, they made messes, they kept the men awake. He approved of this rule, Leo reiterated, and had always upheld it. But tonight he had pleaded with Andy Ragatz to make an exception. The night was so cold, and Jonesy had no place to go. At that very moment the weatherman on the radio was predicting with relish that the temperature would be ten below zero by morning. "He'll freeze to death," said Leo.

C.J. stopped typing and turned around. "He can't stay here."

"We haven't got room," Neal pointed out.

"We have the floor here," said Leo pleadingly. Neal was stunned. He was really serious about letting this stinking wretch sleep in their home.

C.J. took charge. "He can't stay here. It's out of the question. Use your common sense, man. He's a health hazard." Neal shivered, thinking of lice, or bedbugs, or even worse—a loathsome disease.

"He has nowhere to go," said Leo faintly. He looked gaunt. "We tried to find an open building. You know, a hallway or something. Couldn't find anything. He's lame, too. He couldn't walk any farther."

"He can't stay here," C.J. repeated loudly. "God, Leo, we have our rules too. No overnight guests except with *unanimous* consent. Look, Leo, we have *women* here."

"I know. I know. But he'll freeze to death." He began trying to rouse Jonesy. The stench was overpowering. Even C.J. was obviously reluctant to approach the man and help Leo get him on his feet. But at length he did.

"The shelter will have to take him," C.J. said firmly. "On a night like this they'll have to make an exception."

"They won't. Come on, Jonesy, let's go. Let's get on our way, old boy." Aided by C.J., he got the stupefied man on his feet and out the door.

C.J. and Neal stared at each other, unable to speak. Maggie

burst out of her room and rushed to the kitchen cabinet for disinfectant, bug spray, and deodorizer. "Open the windows!" she cried. "The smell is horrible." She began spraying the rug where Jonesy had been lying, while C.J. pounded and pushed at the windows to get them open.

Neal remembered Jake, probably awake and hearing all the turmoil, uncertain whether to get up and put on his prostheses. She went to his door and opened it a crack. The light was on. "Are you awake?" she asked softly.

"Don't come in, Neal. I'm getting up." She could hear the stamping sound that meant he was settling into his foot.

"Don't get up. The crisis is over." Standing at the cracked door she told him the story.

"Oh God," he sighed. "Poor Leo."

Leo did not come home all night. Neal and C.J. stayed up waiting for him until after two. Even after she finally went freezing to bed, Neal kept listening for his return. She woke from a heavy sleep when the first light entered her room. On her way to the bathroom she saw that Leo's bed had not been slept in. C.J. was not in his rumpled bed either. She found him in the kitchen, standing at the sink with a cup of coffee in his hand.

"He didn't come home?" she asked.

"God, what kind of Christians are we?" C.J. asked fiercely.

"Yeah." Neal sank into a chair by the kitchen table in her flannel nightgown. She hadn't even combed her hair. C.J. poured her a mug of coffee and they drank in silence. In a few minutes Jake's door opened and he jerked out on his aluminum canes. He had his legs on and his corduroy pants, but otherwise he looked touseled. He had a sweater over his pajama top, and his hair stood up in back.

"Didn't Leo come home?" Neal couldn't remember his ever appearing before them undressed and ungroomed.

They called the men's shelter but Leo hadn't been seen since he left last night.

At that moment the front door opened and he came in. He looked white, exhausted, utterly distraught, but he managed a ghastly smile. Neal flew to him and embraced him.

"Oh, Leo, forgive us. Forgive me! Thank God you're back. Here, sit down. My God, you're shaking all over."

C.J. handed him a mug of coffee and gripped his shoulder. Leo, still in his down jacket, held his trembling hands around the

113

hot mug, raised it to his lips, but set it down again without taking a sip.

"Where did you go? What happened?" They were all hanging over him anxiously, including Maggie who had now joined them.

Leo spoke slowly, with long pauses between phrases. He told them that he and Jonesy had started back toward the shelter, very slowly because of Jonesy's lameness. Leo had been looking out for a hallway into which Jonesy could creep, but he had found none. A police car had providentially come along, and Leo hailed it, hoping to get Jonesy taken to the police station. But as soon as they got into the car, the cop said Jonesy smelled like gangrene, and he drove immediately to the emergency room of St. Joseph's Hospital. The cop was right: Jonesy had such an advanced case of gangrene that the emergency room surgeon had amputated both his feet immediately. Leo had stayed there until the operation was over and Jonesy had been wheeled back to the ward.

They stared at Leo in silent horror. Jake, balanced on his canes, turned so white that Neal feared he would faint. She moved a chair near him but he did not sit. Maggie smoothed Leo's wild curls.

"So you guys were right," Leo said. "Jonesy couldn't stay here." He breathed a sigh that seemed to come from the core of his being.

"Oh, Leo, you look exhausted," Maggie cried. "You've been through a terrible night. You must eat something." She dropped bread into the toaster. "Would you like scrambled eggs?" She took out eggs and orange juice.

"No, no. Nothing, Mag. I'll just drink this coffee." He took the smallest sip and put the mug down. He looked around at his anxious and disheveled family and again tried a smile. "Listen, I'm sorry I upset you guys." In a babble, they reassured him: the remorse was all on their side. Maggie buttered the toast, in spite of his refusal, and urged him to eat. When he put a piece to his mouth, his face broke into a sweat. He stood up suddenly and headed for the bathroom. They stared at one another, appalled, as they heard him retching.

After a few minutes they heard the toilet flush, and Leo came back to apologize. "Sorry about that. Sorry, Maggie. I guess I won't eat anything right now. I think I'll lie down for a while."

Leo was heavily asleep by the time the rest of them had fin-

114

ished their coffee. Maggie threw the toast in the garbage; nobody felt like eating. They tiptoed around, getting washed and dressed and ready to go to their jobs, but C.J. reported that there was no need to be silent. "He's really out. He'll probably sleep all day. I'll go over to the shelter and report."

Maggie had volunteered to sort clothes at Good Will that day, so there would be nobody at home to disturb Leo. Neal went off to St. Vincent's, her heart heavy. As it turned out, they had been right in refusing to let Jonesy stay the night in their living room, yet Neal burned with remorse for them all. Though their action had been justified, their hearts had been wrong. She didn't know what they should have done, but she had the disturbing conviction that when they had sent Leo and Jonesy out into the freezing night, they had sent Christ out.

On the way home that night Neal stopped at the "all-natural" bakery to buy a loaf of the bread that Leo liked. The purchase left her with less than two dollars, and the end of the month a week away, but she wanted to make some offering to Leo. When she got home she found Maggie working on a similar offering: she was putting Leo's favorite vegetable casserole into the oven.

"He's not here," Maggie reported with a worried frown. "I hope he'll come home for dinner."

Jake came in with a bunch of daffodils for the table.

"I thought you were broke," Neal said.

"I borrowed five bucks from Father Corley."

C.J. brought home a bottle of wine. They laughed sadly at these evidences of their self-recrimination. They set the table and waited for Leo.

He came at last. He still looked gaunt but his color was better. He told them that he had slept nearly all day, but had gone over to the hospital in the late afternoon to visit Jonesy. He laughed as he told them about Jonesy in the hospital.

"That crazy guy is enjoying himself! He was sitting up in bed with his dinner tray, gobbling up everything in sight. He wanted me to sneak him a pint of booze."

"Does he realize—?" Jake didn't complete his question.

"He knows about his feet. But I guess he hasn't thought it through. He's carefree, you know. He doesn't think beyond today."

They sat down to dinner and Leo was touched by all the things they had done to please him. He ate some of Maggie's casserole, not a large helping. He drank a little wine. He praised the all-natural bread, and the daffodils. "Reminds you of spring coming," he said wistfully. He looked sorrowful, even when he smiled.

After dinner they sat around the table and talked about what had happened. Leo acknowledged that they had been right and he had been absolutely wrong the night before. He had shown no prudence, no wisdom, no common sense in bringing Jonesy into the house. He had not been sensitive to the welfare of their community. Moreover he had not even been sensitive to the urgency of Jonesy's condition.

"I don't have good judgment," Leo said. "I don't fit into community life. Maybe I've got to be a kind of bum myself."

"What do you mean? What are you saying?" Their alarmed questions tumbled out.

"I think I ought to leave you guys and—I don't know—live by myself. Be a sort of transient. When you're part of a community you have to live by community rules. It's only right. But that can conflict—I mean, like last night. See, I was identifying with Jonesy instead of with you. I felt like I *had* to."

"You were right, Leo," Neal said passionately. "Maybe you didn't have good judgment, but you had the right *feeling*. You saw Christ in Jonesy. And we didn't."

"Christ is in everybody. You have to balance—sometimes— the good of one against the good of others. Communities have to do this. Even the shelter does. If I had been in charge of the shelter I'd have had to turn Jonesy away. But, I don't know—I feel like I have to act with the outcast. Maybe *be* an outcast. Not have any obligations to any communities. I know this is weird but it feels to me like this is what I have to do."

"But, Leo, the shelter—they need you there," Neal protested, and they all joined. "You're caring for a whole bunch of outcasts. Isn't it better to have some rules so you can keep twenty or thirty men from freezing to death? What good would it do for *you* to freeze to death on the street?"

And they entreated Leo not to leave them. They were in it together for a year, and to break up before the year was over would mean that they had *all* failed. They said the same things they had said to Maggie only days before.

"Let's pray about it," C.J. urged.

Their prayers that evening were deeper and more wrenching than they had ever been before, as they asked God to forgive them for their hardness of heart and cure their poison of selfishness.

"I'm so ashamed," Maggie said, "when I think of how I ran for the bug spray. That's all I was thinking of. Not a scrap of pity for that human being. Christ, have mercy on me."

"I should have gone out with Leo and Jonesy," C.J. said. "Helped Leo take care of him. Why didn't I? Selfishness. Coldness. Lord, have mercy on me."

They prayed for healing and wisdom for Leo and for them all. They prayed for Jonesy, whom they had rejected, that he would be healed and cared for.

"I'll go and see him in the hospital," Jake said. "Maybe I can help him adjust—to amputation."

Neal realized what an offer this was: Jake was identifying himself with the outcast too.

"Don't go away from us," they begged Leo, just as they had begged Maggie.

He agreed to try it for a while longer.

13

As the old axiom promised, March went out like a lamb. Warm winds blew across the plains and the sun beat down and Chicago warmed up. Suddenly the bushes around the front stoop of the flat were putting out buds, and the grass in the narrow front yard was green. The black ice had melted from streets, and even the puddles it left had dried.

Neal, invigorated by the season, stepped up her visits to temporary and permanent job agencies that might have something for her clients. She noticed again the ad in the *Tribune* for a receptionist in an osteopath's office. "Must be good typist. Some bookkeeping helpful." Something about it nagged at her, even though Janie Rawls had predicted that she could never get a receptionist job and Neal had tacitly agreed with her. Obviously the doctor was having some trouble filling it; perhaps it wasn't so easy to find a good typist who also had bookkeeping skill. Neal wondered if she should go to see the doctor on Janie's behalf and sound him out about his requirements for the personal appearance of his receptionist. She had the address printed in her mind, and one day when she was in the neighborhood she entered the building and went up in the elevator. She stood outside the door of Dr. Findlay's office for a few minutes, then slipped in and sat in one of the chairs, as though she had come as a patient. There was no one at the receptionist's desk. About half a dozen patients waited, middle-aged and old people, mostly staring into space concentrating on their ills. A woman leaning on a cane hobbled out of the consulting room, and the doctor followed her and called the next patient. He had a kind face, Neal thought, mildly humorous, as though he would urge people not to take their pains too seriously. He caught sight of Neal and, motioning his patient to proceed into the other room, he picked up a medical history form from the desk and offered it to Neal with a questioning gesture.

"Hello. I haven't seen you before, have I?"

"No. Excuse me, doctor, I'm not a patient. I came to speak to you about your ad for a receptionist." His face lit up and Neal quickly added: "I mean, for a friend of mine. Not for me."

He turned to the patient who was waiting at the door of his consulting room. "Please go in, Mrs. Levy. And please excuse me for just five minutes." Then he motioned to Neal to come around into the receptionist's room where he could talk to her. "I'm very anxious to get a girl for this job. Is your friend working now? Is she a good typist? Tell me about her."

Neal lauded Janie Rawls's typing skill, reported that in the Ferguson Business College she had been the top student in the bookkeeping class, described her self-discipline and motivation. She paused, distrusting the wisdom of calling attention to Janie's major drawback.

"And?" prompted the doctor, with his pleasant twinkle. "What's the fly in the ointment? She sounds too good to be true. Does she want two thousand a month?"

"She's not terribly attractive looking—I mean, for a receptionist."

He laughed. "This is not an advertising office."

"No, but—well, she's rather strange-looking, actually. Until you get used to her. She's got very short legs compared to the rest of her body."

"She'd be sitting at the desk, mostly."

"And rather a big head—"

"Why don't you have her come in and see me? My patients are kind of cramped and crippled, as you've noticed. I don't need a beauty queen sitting here to taunt them. Good typing, some bookkeeping skill, and a person who is careful about records. That's what I need. Tell your friend to come in. And soon."

The next day Janie Rawls had a job.

"I have to wear a white uniform," she told Neal importantly when she came back to the Center with the news. "Dr. Findlay pays for it. He has an account with Acme Uniforms Company. He told me to go over and pick out two and charge them." Her homely face was almost transformed as she spoke of Dr. Findlay's billing system, Dr. Findlay's IBM Selectric Typewriter, Dr. Findlay's office hours, and Dr. Findlay's devotion to his patients. Obviously Janie was already a convert to the value of osteopathy as a treatment for a long list of diseases. "And my uniforms can be either dresses or pants suits," she said finally. "He leaves it up to me—whatever I think looks best."

Everybody at St. Vincent's rejoiced. All the Company of Barnabas rejoiced. Mr. Ferguson, behind his matter-of-fact facade, betrayed a gleam of satisfaction when he saw Neal the next day. "The doctor got a good employee," he said. "When he called me, I told him he was a lucky man."

"I hope you realize, Mr. Ferguson, how much of this is due to you," Neal said. "Giving Janie free tuition, and training her so well, and encouraging her, and giving her references. I hope you feel pleased with yourself. You ought to! You're a good man, Mr. Ferguson."

He waved aside her praise, but he did look a little pleased.

Neal's father had a business meeting in Chicago in early April and her mother came with him. Since Neal wouldn't be coming to visit them at Easter, Dot O'Connor said, they'd have to come to her. Joe O'Connor wanted Neal to invite all her roommates to have dinner with them. He planned to take them to Carson's for sirloin steaks, which he knew they must be craving after nine months of eating "weeds and seeds." But Neal insisted that her parents come to the flat for dinner instead. She knew that a sirloin steak at Carson's would be an obscenity to Leo, and C.J. would probably tell her father exactly how many poor people could be fed for a week on the tab he would pay. "I want you to see how we live, and to meet my roommates in their own setting. It'll be more natural."

Maggie outdid herself on manicotti. Jake made bread. His knee had healed and he no longer had to swing around on elbow canes. He seemed to feel very dashing, as he went about charming her mother with a smooth blend of respect and gallantry. C.J. actually shaved before dinner, and curbed his tongue when her father mentioned Reaganomics in favorable terms.

For their part, Dot and Joe O'Connor were at pains, obviously, to be tactful. They were complimentary about the dinner and the flat; they listened with seeming interest to Leo's stories of comic doings at the shelter (which didn't include any reference to Jonesy); they inquired about FANA's projects without asking any inflammatory questions. They beamed on their clever daughter who was turning out to be such a successful employment counselor. When Joe O'Connor showed signs of wanting to know, from all of them, how all these activities were to be "applied" in the "real world," Dot O'Connor asked Jake to sing. He obliged and they rounded out the evening by a songfest flatteringly rich in the great songs of the fifties. "Do you know 'Wish You Were Here' "? Joe asked. Jake played it while Joe and Dot reached for each other's hands and looked misty. "Our song," said Joe.

The next night Neal had dinner with her parents at their hotel—the last night of their stay. They liked her friends, they told her, Jake especially. "A very talented kid," said her father. "Too bad that he—" Her mother sighed. "And so handsome. What a tragedy."

Neal didn't like their pity. "It's not a tragedy. Jake's conquered it. I don't call it a tragedy when somebody overcomes his handicap and lives a good life."

"Well, yes, he's doing lots of good," Neal's mother conceded gently. "But he can't do all that he could have done. He can't really live a normal life."

"Why not? What do you mean by a normal life?"

"Well, he probably can't marry. I presume that his accident—"

"He's not impotent."

"How do you know?" demanded her father in a loud voice.

"He told me." Surely that was what Jake had meant when he said, "I'm still a man, Neal."

"Neal, how did he happen to tell you that?" Her mother's tone was very anxious.

"We're all sisters and brothers. We talk about *everything*." But had *that* been a brotherly confidence?

120

"I can't imagine your brother Tony discussing a subject like that with you," her father grumbled.

"You'd be surprised the things Tony and I talk about." And that at least was the truth!

Her mother, reassured by the notion of brothers and sisters, was ready to smooth over the tension.

"I like your friends very much, all of them. They're fine young people. It's really inspiring, the way you've all given a year of your lives. You've grown, I'm sure, because of it. You'll get even more out of law school, Neal, after this experience."

"I may not go to law school next year," said Neal cautiously. "I've been offered a job at the Center."

"The Center?"

"St. Vincent's Center. Where I work now. A regular job on the staff. I haven't decided yet, though."

"What kind of job?" asked her father.

"The same thing I do now. Finding jobs for women who have finished their treatment. Helping them develop job skills. Counseling them. The Center is adding twenty beds and we're getting more women patients."

"Spend another year doing the same thing you're doing now? Doesn't sound like progress."

"I'm *developing* the employment program. I've done a lot with it already. I've found some good jobs for some of our women."

"I wish you'd find a good job for yourself." Her father said it in a teasing way, but there was something harsh and hurt in his tone. "What's the salary?"

Neal evaded the question. She spoke instead about the immense satisfaction the job gave her, the thrill she experienced when she could help a woman climb back to self-respect. "When I saw Janie Rawls in her white uniform that she wears in the doctor's office, I just felt so—I can't even express it. It was so exciting! Money couldn't pay me for that thrill."

Her father argued reasonably that job satisfaction was not incompatible with a good income. A lawyer, for example, would experience thrills such as Neal described when he won freedom for an innocent defendant, or—he found a more apt example—got a slum landlord convicted. A doctor surely had his moments of exaltation that had nothing to do with his lucrative practice. Even a stodgy old car salesman—Joe O'Connor owned an Oldsmobile-Buick dealership—got a thrill when the new models came out. Most

121

jobs had these occasional exciting peaks, plus many daily head-aches.

"But in what I do," Neal said, "there's a sort of peace, or thank-fulness, or something, even when things are going badly. I see a lot of misery around me all the time, and yet—I don't know—I feel sort of serene. When I wake up in the morning I feel alive and eager to get the paper and see what jobs there are, and to go to Unemploy-ment and see what's new there, and help my clients fix themselves up for interviews, and practice what they're going to say. And when things turn out badly, and they often do, I feel crushed, but only for a while. Pretty soon I'm up again."

"That's your nature, darling," said her mother fondly. "You've always had such a sunny disposition."

Her father nodded. "You can get job satisfaction in a lot of ways. The point is, now, to make some career plans. Let's take it for granted that you like to help people. That's your basic drive. You can do that, and a lot more effectively, as a lawyer. And earn a good living too. Or you could become a psychologist. They make a very good living, and they're helping people all day long, every day."

It seemed to Neal that they had said all these things before. "Even if I stay another year at the Center, I could still go back to school later."

"What I'm afraid of, Neal," her father said in a grave, porten-tous tone, "is that you'll be stuck in a blind alley. As your mother said, we're proud of your idealism. But if you go on like this for an-other year, and maybe another—I'm afraid you're going to be ru-ined for life. You'll never be able to fit in—"

Neal laughed. "Ruined! Oh, Daddy, that's funny. Sounds like I'm on drugs. Or doing prostitution. Come on, Dad." She glanced back and forth from her mother to her father, trying to coax a smile at the absurdity.

"I'm serious, Neal. I mean *ruined*. I mean wasting your talents and your education and your idealism on amateurish projects. Mak-ing yourself unfit for the real world, where money and professional competence get things done. Don't despise money, Neal. It takes money and professional skill to really help the unfortunates of our society."

"Well, anyway, I haven't made any decision yet."

Neal was depressed after this talk with her parents, but, as usual, not for long. She was planning an Easter party for the residents of St. Vincent's Center: another sing-along. Ever since New Year's people had been asking when Jake would come back and do another concert. Many of those who had been at the New Year's party had left the Center, but the party lived on in legend. Neal and Jake had prepared song sheets containing "Easter Parade," "My Sweet Little Alice Blue Gown," and other old songs the residents could probably sing; Maggie had boiled eggs and colored them. The sing-along would take place on Saturday evening about nine. Before that, Jake had to direct the adult choir at St. Stephen's in the Easter Vigil Mass. The four other sisters and brothers went together to the whole two-hour liturgy, the longest in the Church year. It was a sort of affirmation of their communal spirit, which had been sorely tested of late. All of them seemed to feel they must actively support one another.

"The choir sounded really good. You've done a lot with them," they all told Jake afterward in the sanctuary, where Father Corley was also complimenting him. Father Corley even shook hands with C.J., whom he had scarcely spoken to since the incident of C.J.'s arrest. Then Maggie and Leo and C.J. went off on foot toward the flat, while Neal and Jake got into his car for the drive to St. Vincent's. They had the guitar and the Easter eggs, and the paper napkins in the trunk.

"I don't think you'll have any trouble with lechery tonight," Neal giggled. "Grace Forrester has her own apartment now. Of course she *might* drop in, if she knows you're coming."

They couldn't find a place to park near the Center. Across the street a building was being gutted and a wooden sidewalk detour jutted out into the street, eliminating all parking on that side. They circled the block several times, hoping a spot would open. Then they widened the circle to two blocks.

"There's a parking lot down that alley," Neal said. "Just a little one, for Baylor's drugstore. The store's closed, so maybe—" Jake cruised down the alley and found the rocky, uneven lot. There was room for a car and he started to angle in. "But this is so far," Neal protested. "Why don't we drive to the Center and let you out with the guitar and eggs and stuff, and then I'll come back here with the car?" She had driven Jake's car several times and knew how to use the hand controls. But he wouldn't let her do that. It was too dark. The distance wasn't a problem, he insisted. He could easily walk a few blocks, had often done it. "You can carry the guitar," he conceded.

They were getting the guitar out of the trunk when Neal caught sight of a man emerging from an areaway between stores.

"Well, *hello* there!" he called out.

Her heart raced. The lot was so dark and the approaching figure seemed sinister. Then in the yellow light at the back of Baylor's she saw with relief that it was Blaze Curry.

"Hi there, gorgeous!" His speech was slurred and his gait uneven; he carried the telltale paper bag. He had dropped out of the Center in February, come back and started over in March, and now had been out of sight again for several weeks.

"Hello, Blaze." Neal kept her tone cold. No coddling or softness toward drunks. That was the Center's posture.

"If it isn't my old sweetheart!" He came closer, stumbling between cars. Jake had got the guitar free, and slammed the trunk shut. "Well, who's this?" demanded Blaze, seeing him for the first time. "What's the idea of cheating on me, sweetheart?"

"Go away, Blaze. You're drunk. I don't want to talk to you when you're drunk." She turned from him to reach for the guitar. Jake had stepped back to lock the car doors.

"I'm not drunk, Baby. Had a couple, that's all. Wait a minute. I want to talk to you." He took hold of her wrist, so that she dropped the guitar. His grip was insistent.

"Let go, Blaze," she cried angrily, trying to shake it off. Jake came forward on the rocky ground, steadying himself against the car.

"Get out of here. Get lost!" he commanded. He tried to get in front of Neal and push Blaze away.

Blaze turned and without relinquishing either Neal's wrist or his bottle gave Jake a violent shove with his elbow, knocking him down. Then Blaze tightened his hold on Neal and jerked her back between the cars. "I want to talk to you, Baby."

Don't panic, Neal told herself. Keep it cool. A drunk can't do you much harm. Use your head. "Now, Blaze, let's stop here," she said, trying to control her breathing. She grabbed a car mirror and held on, but had to let go because of the strength of his hold. "Blaze, please, you're hurting my arm. Please let's stop."

"Get away from her!" shouted Jake. "Let her go."

Blaze didn't speak. He just dragged her with relentless force. She stumbled along, unable to free herself. She saw with horror that he was heading toward the areaway from which he had emerged. She struggled to stay calm. You can't be raped by a drunk, she told

124

herself. He would have to let go of her wrist. She'd get him off balance and then make a fast break.

"Get away from her, you bastard." Jake's voice came from farther away.

As she was dragged into the areaway, Neal heard the bottle in Blaze's bag knock against the brick wall and break. Then she realized with despair that he probably had in his hand the neck of a broken bottle.

It was very dark. She felt herself thrown to the ground. She didn't know where the bottle was. She wouldn't test it. She tried no more pleading. Blaze didn't speak. He mauled and tore, and she did what was required. The transaction was wordless, fast, and bestial. From an immense distance she heard Jake still calling, "I'm coming Neal!"

Blaze rolled away from her. She heard his hard breathing and smelled the stink of him. She lay without moving as she felt rather than saw him struggle to his feet and stumble off down the areaway away from the lot. An absurd thought flashed across her mind: he didn't even say goodbye.

When he was out of hearing, she felt cautiously on the ground around her for broken glass. She touched the wet paper bag and realized that the broken bottle was still inside. Keeping clear of that, she got heavily to her feet. Her body didn't seem to be her own. As she pulled her clothes to order she felt as though she was handling another person.

"Neal!" Jake's piercing voice was much closer. When she ran from the areaway she almost fell over him—he was crawling toward her. In the yellow light she saw that he had only one foot. The right trouser leg dragged empty below the knee.

"Jake, you're hurt!" She flung herself down beside him.

"Oh, Neal." He was panting with effort. "I couldn't get to you. When I went down—my foot—came off. It's stuck—under the car. I couldn't—I thought I could—get to you faster—if I crawled."

"Jake. Jake."

"I couldn't get there fast enough."

"Even if you did—he had a broken bottle."

"Oh God! Did he—"

"He didn't cut me. I didn't fight him."

"Neal, see if you can reach my foot. Under the car. You have to get to the hospital."

At first she couldn't find it. Then a dim reflection from the shoe showed it to her, partly hooked by the car's undercarriage. She had to lie on her stomach to work it free. Then she jumped up and ran back to him, carrying the foot with its shoe and sock, and above the sock the molded hollow calf. Jake had worked his trouser leg up over his right knee, and there was the tapered stump, seamed and scarred and tough-looking. She saw how it would fit into the molded calf. Jake fished into the socket with his hand.

"There's something missing," he said. "A sort of little wool sock—oh, wait I think it's here in my pant leg." He partially unrolled the trouser and brought out what he was looking for: a cap that fit over the stump before it was inserted into the socket. His hands were shaking as he tried to get it on quickly. "It has to be tight," he said. Neal watched him ease the stump into the socket and settle it forcefully, like a man pulling on a boot. Then he pulled down the trouser. He scooted nearer to a parked car and reached up to grab the door handle. Bracing his right heel, he took Neal's hand on the other side and with a powerful jerk he pulled himself upright, gained his balance, and stamped on the foot to settle it firmly. "Good thing it wasn't the left one. Much more complicated," he gasped. They stood there, hands still clasped, shaking and trying to get their breaths.

"We must go right to the hospital," Jake said.

"Shouldn't we call the police?" There was no phone booth to be seen.

"We can do that from the hospital. After all, you know who it was. And I saw him too." They picked their way to the car, retrieved the guitar and jammed it into the trunk.

"You're bleeding," Neal cried, when the inside car lights came on. There was blood on the collar of Jake's jacket and in his hair behind his ear.

He fingered the place gingerly and then wiped his hand on his trousers. "It doesn't hurt. I must have hit a rock when I fell." He turned to her with a look of anguish. "Do *you* hurt much?"

"I'm numb." He turned on the ignition and they drove out of the lot.

In the emergency room at Bethel-Kemp Hospital Neal gave her report first to a receptionist, and then to a policeman, who made notes on a form, and asked questions. Do you know his address? No, but the St. Vincent's Center might have it. Did he threaten you? Did he show a weapon?

Neal told him about the broken bottle in the bag. "But maybe it wasn't an intentional weapon. I don't know whether he broke it on purpose or if it just happened to—"

The policeman shook his head, contemptuous of such a scruple. "What did *you* do?" he asked Jake.

"Tried to shove him away from her. Couldn't do it." He looked the policeman in the eye. "I'm a double amputee."

"Oh yeah?" The policeman glanced quickly at his legs and then away. His eye caught the blood on Jake's neck and collar. "Did he hit you?"

"No. Knocked me down. I must have hit my head on a rock. Or the fender of the car."

The policeman's manner became more reassuring. He and his partner would track down the "perpetrator" and pick him up. They would go to the scene and try to retrieve the "weapon."

"You'll have to testify in court," he warned Neal.

"Yes."

"You too."

"Yes," answered Jake.

The doctor was a young black woman. She told Neal that she was on gynecological service, and that she had asked the Emergency Room to call her if possible whenever there was a rape case.

She examined Neal, talked to her calmly, explained what she was doing. "Now this will hurt a bit. This will burn for a minute or so." Neal welcomed the burning, as though it could purge her of the shameful event.

"Now you don't have to worry about any *physical* effects," Dr. Brainerd said when she had finished. "Pregnancy, or disease, or infection. We've taken care of all that."

After Neal had dressed, Dr. Brainerd sat with her in a little room and talked about psychological effects. Many women, she said, were oppressed with guilt because they had not resisted the rapist more strongly. "Some of them almost feel they should have resisted to the *death*. That's an old-fashioned, mythical idea that has absolutely no virtue in it. The virtuous thing to do is to minimize the damage as much as you can."

"That's what I did."

"You did right. Absolutely right. Congratulate yourself on that. Don't feel any guilt about it."

She urged Neal not to let herself feel that she had been besmirched or degraded or cheapened. "Nothing that anybody forces on you can change what you *are*," she said. "You are the same person." Neal nodded, trying to feel like the same person. The trouble was, she didn't feel like a person at all. She seemed to be walking through an atrocity that couldn't possibly have anything to do with the fortunate, sunlit life of Neal O'Connor.

Another thing, the doctor continued: Neal must guard against developing hostility and anger against *all* men because of what one man had done to her. Some women, the doctor said, turned cold to their husbands or boyfriends. "Don't let this come between you and your boyfriend. He must have tried very hard to defend you. He's got a nasty wound on his head. Don't feel angry at him because he couldn't help you."

"He did help me!" cried Neal fiercely. "You wouldn't believe how he—he has artificial legs, both of them! He tried to—" A great gulping sob burst from her, and then another, and she couldn't speak anymore. She held her hands over her face, struggling for control.

"It's probably good to cry," Dr. Brainerd said quietly.

But Neal didn't want to make it harder for Jake by breaking down. "I'm all right," she said, giving a little shake. "Really, I feel much better because of what you've said. I'll remember what you've said. You've helped me a lot."

"I want you to call me in a day or two. Nothing official. I just want to see how you're coping psychologically. Will you do that?" She gave Neal her phone number. "You may find it easier to talk to me because I'm a physician, and a stranger, than to talk to the people close to you." Then the doctor gave her a sleeping pill. "This is really strong. Take it right before you get into bed. It will knock you out. When you wake up in the morning there will already be one day between you and this experience. Every day it will be farther away."

"Will you give me one for Jake too? He'll need one. It was just as hard on him as it was on me. Maybe worse."

"Let's see what Dr. Praska says." She led Neal out to the reception room, where Jake was waiting for her with a big bandage around his head. Dr. Praska, the emergency room doctor who had dressed his wound, had already given him a sedative to take when he got home.

Neal's throat closed up again when she saw Jake, so she threw herself into civilities and acknowledgments, thanking the receptionist, shaking hands with Dr. Praska and Dr. Brainerd, and assuring Dr. Brainerd that her care and sensitivity had been an immense comfort. "I'll call you next week," she promised.

Then she took Jake's arm and they went out to the car.

"Look," she said, pointing to a clock on a nearby bank. "It's only ten-thirty. Doesn't it seem—"

"I called the Center," Jake said, "and told them I had had an accident with the car. I thought it would be better not to—"

"Yes."

The car radio played quiet music. They didn't talk much. "Are you all right?" "Yes, are you?" "Yes."

After a while Neal said: "Some guy in Baylor's parking lot is going to have a surprise. I left the box of colored Easter eggs sitting on the hood of his car." She managed a little giggle.

Their brothers and sister took it hard. "I'm ashamed of being a man!" Leo exclaimed bitterly. C.J. paced up and down in a fury, his fists clenched. He wanted to go to the police station and see whether they had arrested Blaze Curry, and to hound them into action if they hadn't, but the rest of them talked him out of it. Maggie could only embrace Neal and Jake, first one and then the other, and sob. "Oh why did this have to happen? Why?" she wailed.

Neal found that she and Jake were doing the comforting and soothing, instead of the other way around. It was as if they had grown old, and the younger ones were clamoring for interpretation and guidance. She felt immensely weary. She longed for a hot, cleansing bath. "Let's say a prayer together," she suggested at length, "and then go to bed." They said the Our Father, just that, and then embraced one another.

The last thing she had to do was to kiss Jake goodnight without weeping.

Then the long bath, and the pill—which worked instantly.

The next day was Easter. Before she was even up, Neal heard Joan Kinsella's voice. The police had come to St. Vincent's the night before to inquire about Blaze Curry, and Joan had heard the news that morning when she arrived at the Center. She came into Neal's bedroom with a bunch of tulips in her hand, looking utterly stricken. Neal had never expected to see that stoic, calm face so roiled with anger and pain. That the outrage should have been committed by an alcoholic from the Center was devastating to her. "I

129

always suspected Blaze had a yen for you," she moaned. "But I never dreamed—"

"What could you do? You can't have a man locked up because you suspect he has a yen for somebody. Don't feel responsible. You're not responsible. The Center's not responsible. It's just something that happened."

"Alcohol is responsible, that curse, that poison. If Blaze had been sober he would never have—"

"Or if he'd been drunker he *couldn't* have." But Neal could not coax even a grim smile out of Joan.

Leo and Maggie were cooking an Easter breakfast. They put Joan's tulips on the table as a centerpiece and made her stay. She must meet the rest of the family: Jake emerged with his bandaged head, and C.J. appeared freshly shaved and wearing a clean shirt.

"What an original Easter bonnet, Jake!" exclaimed Neal. It was a feeble joke, but she had to try something to brighten the troubled faces around the table.

Jake took her message and began to sing, "In my Easter bonnet, with all the blood upon it, I'll be the grandest hero in the Easter parade." But Neal could see what a strain it was for him.

Adrenalin, or nervous energy, or whatever it is that helps people to rise to unaccustomed heights of fortitude at the time of a shock, helped Neal get through that day. Inside her there was a cistern full of tears, dammed up, throbbing to be released, but she must keep the cover tight because of Jake. She was breezy and vivacious. She didn't meet anyone's eye for fear of a stab of sympathy. Especially she avoided looking at Jake. If their glances were to lock she might not be able to contain her flood.

Jake tried, they all did, to be easy and natural. After they had gone to Mass together, they sat around the living room, passing the Sunday papers back and forth, commenting with artificial interest on the news items. Nobody wanted to go out—it was raining anyway. They seemed to want to stay together, and yet they couldn't talk about the one thing that was on their minds. Neal's attitude forbade them to talk about it. She was afraid of what it would do to Jake.

She knew he was suffering. How could he not suffer? A fearful outrage had been committed against her and he had not been man enough to prevent it—that would be the knife in his heart. She had to make as little of the outrage as possible, and keep the others from making much of it.

She kept reminding herself of what Dr. Brainerd had told her, that each day there would be a little more distance between her and what had happened. For Jake, too, each day would put his humiliation farther away, especially if nobody spoke of it. If she could only go somewhere alone and weep without restraint, for hours—but that was impossible.

When the miserable day at last came to an end, Neal went to her bed with a bitter relief. But, lying in the dark, she began to see that it was wrong not to talk to her sisters and brothers about her sorrow. Silence would separate her from them, especially from Jake. She resolved that she would open the subject, and that resolution brought her an unexpected feeling of lightness. When she awoke early in the morning she had a new outlook.

"Listen, you guys," she said, having lingered over her coffee until they were all in the kitchen at the same moment. "I think there's a meaning in what happened to me." She tried to speak briskly. "Something I didn't see right away. We've all been trying to identify with the poor, haven't we? Well, now we really have identified with the poor. The poor live all the time with things like this, violence, brutality. With dark stairs, abandoned buildings, and vacant lots all around them. And unsafe hallways. The poor are vulnerable all the time. Even the children. Now I know more about them. More about what their lives are like."

They nodded. Yes, they saw what she meant. It was true: in their safe middle-class lives there were gaps of understanding that reading and studying and even sustained social action could never fill in. Violence could teach them a harsher knowledge of the sufferings of the poor than they had yet, with all their good intentions, been able to learn.

"And the husbands and fathers of the poor," Neal went on, looking steadily at Jake, "they have to live with it. They can't keep their families safe. Can't protect them. That's what it is to be poor. We're deeper into it now."

Jake bowed his head in acknowledgment of what she had said. A dreadful sadness seemed to have settled on him, which she couldn't penetrate.

"Will you drive me to the Center this morning?" she asked him a few minutes later. She usually went on the bus, or walked if the weather was nice.

131

"Drive somewhere," she said when they were in the car. "To Lincoln Park or somewhere. We have to talk." Without speaking he drove to the park, and they got out of the car and walked along a path, holding each other by the hand, still in silence. They came to a bench and sat down.

"Tell me what you're feeling," Neal said.

"Can't you imagine?"

"Maybe, but I want you to tell me."

"I couldn't save you. I couldn't defend you."

"But you were heroic! I'll never forget the way you tried to come to me, bleeding, and on your knees."

"But I couldn't save you. That's what's killing me."

"I know it's killing you. But let me tell you how it looks to me. It looks to me as if you and I suffered *equally* in this. This event, this suffering, belongs to us both. We went through it together. We *own* it, you and I. And when people go through something terrible together it forges a bond."

Jake bowed his head, his hands over his face. "Oh, Neal," he cried brokenly.

The flood-gate inside her burst. She put her arms around Jake and sobbed against his coat, feeling his sobs shaking them both. An occasional jogger shot them a curious look, diagnosing a lover's quarrel probably. Neal felt as though she would never get to the bottom of her tears. They kept coming. Once she thought she was finished and then the torrent began again. Jake got control of himself first. He held her and smoothed her hair. He didn't speak.

At last Neal grew calmer. "I'm not crying for myself, really. I'm crying because *you* are suffering so much. I wanted to try to make you see," she hiccuped, "that we have to share this thing. It belongs to us both. My pain is your pain and yours is mine."

He gave her a weak smile. "I'll try to see it that way." He struggled to his feet and went over to a nearby drinking fountain, where he soaked his handkerchief to help her bathe her swollen eyes. She fumbled for a mirror in her handbag.

"Oh my God, look at me. I can't go to the Center like this." She peered at Jake. "And you look terrible too. Father Corley will think you've been boozing all weekend. What'll we do? It'll take hours for this face of mine to get back to normal."

"No, it won't. We'll get some coffee and doughnuts. We'll be okay in a while."

"Let's go to a takeout place. I can't bear to go in anywhere looking like this."

So they stopped at a little food shop and Jake went in and got coffee and doughnuts to go, and they ate them in the car, not saying much, watching the people going to work in the April sunshine.

Finally Neal got to work on her face, wiped the powdered sugar from her mouth, touched it with lipstick, and fluffed her hair. Jake watched, gravely attentive. "Do I look more or less normal now?" she asked.

"Yes, normal. Beautiful," he murmured as he started the car.

14

*T*he five of them drew closer. Leo said no more about leaving them; Maggie went about her various neighborly offices with seeming content. Their spirits seemed almost to lighten, as though the harsh trials they had endured had freed them. They could laugh and tease one another without skirting around touchy subjects. Jake no longer kept his bedroom door closed at night. And several times Neal noticed that C.J. shaved in the bathroom while Jake took his shower.

Maggie marveled at Neal's resilience. "I don't know how you can do it, Neal," she said one night when they were lying in bed. "I admire you *enormously*. If that had happened to me, I'd be a wreck. I know I would."

"I'm not as stoic as you think. I totally fell apart with Jake one day. Cried for an hour."

"But you keep up. You go to work. You even laugh. I don't think I could. I don't know if I could ever get over it."

"The thing is, Mag," Neal mused, "that when I think of that night, I don't—I mean I hardly ever—think of that dark alley and that filthy man. The picture that stays with me is Jake, Jake crawling between the cars—without his foot, Mag—trying to reach me and save me. All the while it was happening, Mag, he kept calling out to me,' I'm coming Neal.' That's what is vivid, Mag."

Maggie gave a little moan of understanding.

At St. Vincent's Center the residents overwhelmed Neal with

vociferations of their affection and support for her, and with vengeful imprecations against Blaze Curry. They were gleeful when they heard that Blaze was in jail: he should stay there; he should rot there; he should be sentenced for life; he should hang. Dan, the cook, declared darkly that even hanging was too good for him: he should be "dismembered." Center residents hadn't been so lively and so united for a long time. Neal longed for the subject to fade and for the uncomfortable attention to move away from her. But it couldn't, as long as Blaze's trial still loomed, an event to be dreaded like a necessary operation.

Residents who had finished their treatment and gone on to jobs and independence heard about Blaze's crime at their AA meetings. Many of them dropped in to sympathize with Neal—and of course to gossip about the event. It turned out that everybody had known all along that Blaze Curry was a rotter. Mrs. Schorski had spotted him as a "prevert" the very first time she had laid eyes on him. Janie Rawls said he always gave her the creeps.

Janie came in on her lunch hour one day, in her white pants suit, and brought Neal a present to comfort her. It was a bottle of cologne called June Meadows, an overpowering scent.

"It was so thoughtful of Janie," Neal remarked to Maggie, as she sprayed herself liberally the next morning. "But isn't it *piercing?*"

C.J. sniffed with disgust when Neal came into the kitchen for coffee. "What have you been dousing yourself with? God, that's terrible!"

"Janie Rawls gave it to me. I think it was so sweet of her."

"It smells like a brothel." C.J. poured Neal's coffee.

"How many brothels have you patronized, Clarence?"

"You don't have to wear it just because she gave it to you. Will you see her today?"

"No, but she gave it to me. I have to accept her present. It's like Mrs. Rivera's pie."

Their neighbor, Mrs. Rivera, had made them an apple pie. Maggie had been helping her cook and shop and repair her children's clothes, and Mrs. Rivera had expressed her gratitude by making a pie for Maggie's household. It was the most deplorable pie any of them had ever encountered.

"Why is it so *gummy?*" asked Jake, poking at his piece with distaste.

"Mrs. Rivera probably put too much cornstarch in it," Maggie said. "She's good at making tacos and enchiladas, but she wanted to make something 'Anglo' for us. It was very thoughtful of her." Maggie doggedly chewed.

C.J. wanted to throw it in the garbage. "Mrs. Rivera doesn't see our garbage. She won't know."

Neal supported him. "You can tell her we ate it. That's not a lie. We did all eat *some* of it." Most of it was still on their plates, and a third of it in the pie tin.

Maggie declared that they must eat it all. It wasn't a question of whether Mrs. Rivera would know, it was a matter of accepting a present that had been given to them. "We mustn't do all the giving," Maggie said. "We must also take. If our neighbors give us a present of food, we must eat it. We mustn't feel superior to their gift. To look down on their gift is to look down on *them*."

They submitted and ate the pie. Maggie served the remaining portion at their next meal, and they had to eat another narrow slice.

Thus Neal, in the same spirit, set off for work reeking of June Meadows. That day she told Joan Kinsella that she would take the counseling job at St. Vincent's Center, beginning in July.

Jake was giving Leo a haircut, while Neal sat by, waiting her turn for a trim.

"I'm going to be a Domer, Neal," Jake said as he snipped.

"What?"

"I'm going to Notre Dame this summer. For a program in liturgy. I'll be a Domer."

"This summer?"

"Notre Dame has a summer workshop in liturgy. Father Corley wants me to go to it. He's going to pay for it."

"Hey, man, that's super!" cried Leo.

"Father Corley's hiring me as parish music coordinator. He wants me to go down to Notre Dame and participate in this workshop and see what good things are being done in liturgy, and then maybe adapt some of them to our parish."

"Jake, that's marvelous!" Neal exclaimed. "And you thought Father Corley wanted to get rid of you."

"I was wrong. He likes what I've done. He's proud of the choir. He thinks it's been good for parish life. He wants to start a teenage choir, with guitars and flutes. But it must be liturgically sound. That's why he wants me to go to Notre Dame. To learn good liturgical practice."

135

"Wait till C.J. hears this," said Leo. "He thinks Corley is an old dinosaur."

"He's still conservative. He's already warned me: no jukebox hymns. No liturgical dance!"

Leo's cut was finished and Neal took her place on the stool. "So you'll be living in Chicago next year, Jake?"

"Yeah, I'll have to find an apartment." He was combing and dividing her hair, preparing to trim. "A cheap apartment. Music coordinator is not one of your highest-paid professions."

"I'll be staying in Chicago too." Neal dropped her little firecracker nonchalantly, waiting to see them jump. "I'm joining the staff of St. Vincent's." She told them that Joan had offered her a regular job, starting in July, to continue and expand the job counseling with women residents. "So I'll be looking for a cheap apartment, too."

"Hey that's so cool," Leo said, laughing at the wonderful coincidence. "The two of you. That's really cool."

Jake just stared at her, his face a wordless alleluia. The moment expanded, sucked in the future, and showed Neal the meaning of all that had happened. ◆